Granny the Pag

Granny the Pag

by NINA BAWDEN

Clarion Books ✧ *New York*

Clarion Books
a Houghton Mifflin Company imprint
215 Park Avenue South, New York, NY 10003
Copyright © 1995 by Nina Bawden
First American edition 1996
The text is set in 13/16-point Centaur.

For information about this and other Houghton Mifflin trade and reference books
and multimedia products, visit The Bookstore at Houghton Mifflin
on the World Wide Web at ⟨http://www.hmco.com/trade/⟩.

Printed in the USA

Library of Congress Cataloging-in-Publication Data
Bawden, Nina, 1925–
Granny the Pag / by Nina Bawden.
p.   cm.
Summary: Originally abandoned by her actor parents who later attempt to gain custody,
Cat wages a spirited campaign to decide her own fate and remain with her grandmother.
ISBN 0-395-77604-X
[1. Grandmothers—Fiction.   2. Parent and child—Fiction.   3. Schools—Fiction.]   Title.
PZ7.B33Gr   1996
[Fic]—dc20   95-38191
CIP
AC

BP   10   9   8   7   6   5   4   3   2

There are a lot of people whose help I would like to acknowledge: judges, solicitors, barristers, guardians-ad-litem, and numerous court officials who have been generous with their time and advice, but who may not, however, wish to be named. But I think I may acknowledge a debt to my granddaughter, Ottilie Kark, who once, long, long ago, was uncertain how to spell *pig*.

—*N.B.*

Granny the Pag

Chapter One

OTHER PEOPLE'S GRANDMOTHERS are soft and powdery and gentle and kind. Like Tom and Rosie's grandmother. But my granny is a Pag.

Rosie is my best friend and Tom is her brother. Their grandmother lives in a pretty house not far from our school, and we usually stop there on our way to the station before we catch the train home. There is always a vase of flowers in the *exact middle* of their grandmother's window, and when she opens the door she always says, "Oh, what a lovely surprise," as if this is the first time she's seen us for about nine hundred years. Perhaps it's silly of her to pretend she wasn't expecting us when she has a tray with three mugs and a plate of biscuits ready and waiting, but it feels nice, all the same.

Granny-the-Pag never comes to the door. I have my own house key and as I come in she just shouts from wherever she is, "Who goes there?" And when I answer, she says, "Pass, friend." If Rosie and Tom are with me and I ask if we can have a Coke, instead of saying, as their grandmother would, "Darling, don't you think milk would be nicer, or fresh lemonade?" the Pag says, "Go ahead, rot your teeth, see if I care."

Tom and Rosie live next door and are used to her, and because they are my friends, I don't think they would say anything behind my back. But I wouldn't want anyone else to come home with me. The house isn't dirty because we have someone to clean it—a different person about every month or so, no one can stand it much longer—but there are a lot of cats, nine last time I counted, and four dogs, all rather old. And, worst of all, the Pag *smokes* and everything smells of it, curtains, carpets, dogs, and cats, as well as my hair!

"It's a dirty and disgusting habit," I tell her. "Look at you, ash all down your front, and a yellow moustache and brown teeth, and what's more you'll die of it if you're not careful. *Green slime* will fill up your lungs and you'll *die.*"

Sometimes, if it's a cold day, she opens a window then and makes me sit right beside it, but mostly she just laughs until she starts coughing. "I'm not aiming to live to a hundred. You wouldn't want me to, either. You might have to look after me, and that would be a penance for both of us."

At least she doesn't smoke when she comes to school, to the prize-giving or the Christmas play. I tell her she needn't come if she really can't bear it, but she has decided it is her duty to stand in for my parents on every occasion of that sort, and so she sits there, usually in the very front row, looking grim.

Weird, too. Rosie's grandmother wears pretty, soft clothes, woolly and silky, in pale colors. She keeps her glasses on a gold chain around her neck, there are tiny gold studs in her ears, and she always smells nice, like violet pastilles or scented soap. But when Granny-the-Pag isn't dressed in her jeans or her motorbike leathers, she wears dusty black skirts that trail on the ground, and she has a horrible fur jacket that she brings out for special occasions. I tell her it's wrong to kill animals just to keep warm or look smart, but she says, "Whichever old wolf this pelt belonged to died so long ago I don't think you need trouble to mourn it. But if it really upsets you, I'll wear the black wool and the Brooch."

Which puts me on the spot. The black wool is one thing—you can't see where the moths have been at it unless you look closely—but the Brooch is a different kind of embarrassment altogether. Proper grandmothers have proper jewelry, pearls and delicate rings, the sort of things they can leave to their granddaughters. The Brooch is enormous, about the size of my clenched fist, a huge chunk of gold covered in birds and flowers made out of diamonds. It belonged to the Pag's grandmother who lived in Russia hundreds of years ago and must have been very rich, unless that kind of thing was much cheaper then. The Pag wears it to hide stains on her sweaters, or to hold her clothes together when a button is lost or a zip broken. She says it has a good strong pin.

My mother once said to her, "My precious darling, you really *must not* wear that great vulgar gewgaw all the time, you'll get *mugged*, my angel." (My mother calls everyone "darling" or "precious," usually because she has forgotten their names, though she must remember her mother's.) But the Pag just shrugged and said, "I doubt anyone would think it was real. Not if they took a good look at the rest of me."

When I was five or six I used to boast at school that my grandmother's family came from Russia and that this big brooch was given to them by the czar. Now I am older (thirteen next birthday), it seems dreadful to wear something so valuable when people are starving in Africa and sleeping on the streets in New York and London. We did a project on Poverty in the Third World last term, and because I finished before anyone else I did an extra essay on Poverty in the West.

And, of course, some people might say that if the Pag sold the Brooch, she could afford to buy herself some decent clothes instead of going around looking like a bag lady or a Raggedy Ann. I expect that is what the girls in my class say behind my back. Along with a lot of other things about my mother and father: how *he* has had false hair woven over the bald patch on top of his head and how *she* has had (or needs) a new facelift.

Before I start the story, I had better explain who I am. My name is Catriona Natasha Brooke. The Natasha comes from my mother, and the Brooke from my father. I suppose I am lucky it was that way around: the Pag's family name, which was my mother's before she married my father, is very long and almost unpronounceable. Catriona is a Scottish name, and I was given it because my parents were on tour in Scotland when I was born. The Pag says my mother gave birth to me during the twenty-minute interval in the middle of the play in the leading lady's dressing room. (My mother wasn't the leading lady, she was only playing the maid, but I was an emergency.)

Some of the teachers at school call me Catriona. Most other people call me Cat, except the Pag sometimes, when she is being very serious, or my mother, if she speaks to me on the telephone. When she has run out of names like *sweetheart* and *dearest* and *jewel* she calls me "Nat-*arrr*-sha," rolling her *r*'s as if she has something tickling her tongue.

I don't know what my parents called me when I was very young. I do know there was a stage before we got to the *darling*s and *angel*s when I was known as the Kid. "Where's the Kid?" "Anyone seen the Kid?" Usually with a rude adjective in front of *Kid*.

That was before the Pag took me over, when I was still being trailed around with my mother and father and the rest of the theater company, sleeping in the hamper that belonged to the wardrobe mistress and being wrapped in a shawl and carried onstage whenever the play called for a baby. I suppose I got too big to be useful in that way. The next thing I knew, I was sitting in a big old armchair, picking at the stuffing that was oozing out of holes in the seat, and the Pag and I were glaring at each other, eyeball to eyeball. I had never seen anyone who looked so tall and so thin. She had a big sharp nose and big sharp eyes that were a very light, piercing ice blue, and her hands were like scarecrow hands, long and twiggy. I must have seen a scarecrow somewhere, perhaps in a picture book. And I must have been scared because I started to bawl and thump my feet up and down in the chair. Then this terrifying scarecrow knelt down in front of me and said, "Hush, hush, little Cat, don't grieve so, it tears my heart out to see you. . . ."

She can't really have said that. So *un*-Pag-like! But it is what I remember. And she wasn't a Pag then, of course.

I couldn't spell, that was how it happened. I could

read, but no one had taught me to listen to how the words sounded before I wrote them down.

I was unhappy. I can't remember missing my mother and father, but I remember that I was frightened. And I was angry with this tall, twiglike person I was supposed to call "Granny." So I shouted at her. I threw my mug of milk at the kitchen wall. I spat out my carrots. She took me shopping and I threw myself on the ground in the middle of Woolworth's and screamed and kicked my heels until a circle of people with red faces stood around, looking down at me, muttering. She gave me a bowl of ice cream for tea and I mashed it and smashed it until it ran in white streams down the edge of the table and puddled on the floor, where the cats licked it. Then I ran up to my room, stomping my feet hard on each stair. I banged my bedroom door open and banged it shut, then opened it so I could slam it again. I wanted to make her sorry. I tore a piece of paper out of my notebook and wrote *Granny is a Pig* and opened the door again and stuck it on the outside with tape.

Only I didn't write *Granny is a Pig.*

I wrote *Granny is a Pag.*

I heard her coming. She tapped on the door. Then she made a funny noise. I thought, *She's seen my notice, she's angry.* I wondered what she would do. Would she kill me? But when I opened the door, she was sitting on the top stair, laughing and laughing. Tears were running down her cheeks.

✧

The Pag is a doctor. Years and years ago, she worked in a hospital in Poland. Then the war came and the hospital was bombed. She rescued as many patients as she could but the hospital was destroyed, so she caught the last train out of Poland, and then the last plane out of somewhere else, and got to England where she married my grandfather. He had escaped from Poland, too. He was a scientist, and he had a job ready for him in America, but he died very suddenly a month before my mother was born, and the Pag got a job at a London hospital and bought a house in the suburbs which is where we live now. She is retired from the hospital but she still sees some of her old patients privately. She doesn't charge them. She says none of them have any money.

Most of the people who come to see her are old (as well as being old patients) and some of them are peculiar. One lady has to have the windows closed and the curtains drawn before she comes into the house in case *someone*— she doesn't say who—might look through the windows and see her. There is a man who talks to himself, listening to himself in between, and laughing as if his second self, the self other people can't hear, has said something unexpectedly funny. Another man smiles all the time but only with his mouth; his eyes look straight ahead, not *at* you but *through* you. That is really unnerving.

Although I am a little afraid of the smiling man, I am

used to these people. But they are another good reason for not bringing people home. I can just hear some of the girls in my class putting it about that Cat Brooke lives in a madhouse! Girls are much meaner than boys in that sort of way. Luckily, apart from Rosie and Tom, no one else from school lives in this part of town, and Rosie and Tom understand about patients because their mother is a doctor, too. She has a surgery built on the back of the house and sometimes she sends the Pag one of her patients who doesn't need medicine, just someone to talk to.

I don't want to be a doctor. (I don't want to go into the theater, either.) But if I did take up medicine, I would be a proper doctor. I said to the Pag once, "The people who come to see you, they never go away, they just keep on coming. Rosie's mother, she hands out medicine and bandages, and her patients get better."

"I'm not very handy with bandages," the Pag said. "And I hate the sight of blood. Besides, if I didn't look after my people, no one else would. Most of them are never going to get any better, but sometimes they feel better for a little while after talking to me." She looked at me, head on one side, blue eyes sharp and bright. "What is it *really*, Cat?"

She makes me jump when she says things like that. She always knows when there is something that I'm not saying. What I had really been thinking was that most of the patients who went to the surgery next door were normal, sensible people who just happened to be ill at that moment. If the Pag's patients were like Rosie's mother's—instead of grubby and weird like old Flossie, who looks as if she sleeps in a hedge, or plain dotty like Mr. Wilberforce Frisbee, who dances up the drive, busily conducting an invisible orchestra—the Pag might smarten herself up and look a bit more ordinary and respectable, a little bit more like a real grandmother. Nobody of her age should have long gray hair flying wild halfway down her back; no one as old as she is should be allowed on a motorbike. It's not safe. There should be a law against it.

Chapter Two

IT HAD BEEN ALL RIGHT in primary school. I had known the Pag was a more noticeable sort of person than other parents or grandparents. I knew that people looked at her in a special way when she came into the playground to fetch me, and that sometimes they smiled secretly at each other when her back was turned. But I didn't mind because of something my teacher had said.

My teacher's name was Hilda, and she was very pretty, with straight, shiny hair, so fair it was almost silvery. It fell on both sides of her face when she bent down, and everyone in our class tried to touch it, to see what it felt like. I suppose we were all in love with her, the way little kids are often in love with their teacher when they first go to school.

Every Monday we had a Bring and Tell lesson—we had to bring a piece of news to school and tell it to the rest of the class. Each week the news had to be about something different: Pets, or Weather, or Holidays. One Monday the news was to be about Families. The first people to put up their hands told the rest of the class what their mother or their father had done that weekend. Rosie's dad had taken her and Tom to the National Science Museum on Saturday and mended the rabbit hutch on Sunday and cooked lunch for everyone while Rosie's mum weeded the garden. I didn't put up my hand but Hilda looked at me in the end and I had to say something.

I said, "I live with my granny."

Several people giggled behind me. Hilda looked at them fiercely. Then she said, smiling at me, "I know, dear, but your granny really *is* your family."

I looked at my desk and clenched my mouth tight. On Sunday, the Pag and I had been out on the bike for what she called "a real old zoom" on the motorway. It was the most exciting thing in the world to be riding pillion, cuddled tight against the Pag's back, my arms locked round her waist, the big powerful bike roaring and swooping and tilting beneath me, and the wind blowing into me and filling my chest. But it wasn't the sort of thing the others had told about and I didn't want to be different.

Hilda said, in a kind voice, "I know your mum and

your dad are famous people, Cat. Lots of people have seen them on television. But your granny is a wonderful person in a way you will understand better when you are older."

She had got it all muddled. She thought I was ashamed because I didn't live with my mother and father. But it didn't matter. She had said the Pag was wonderful. And I could tell by the way she said "famous" that she didn't think so much of my mother and father.

I understood this perfectly well, even though I was only six years old then, too young to have found the words to explain it.

I wriggled on my chair and said, "My Granny is a Pag." I said it very softly because I had never said it aloud before, and Hilda didn't hear me. She was nodding at a boy who had his hand up in the back of the class. And while this boy went boringly on, talking about how his mum had made a birthday cake for his sister and his sister had blown out all her four candles, I said it under my breath, over and over again, like a charm.

My Granny is a Pag.

"What's a Pag?" Rosie asked in the back of the car. (It was her mum's turn to collect us that day.)

"Oh, I dunno," I said. Pretending.

"It sounds *wild*," Tom said. He sniggered, and jabbed

me in the ribs with his elbow, and went red in the face. "Like someone who steals little girls."

"Or eats nasty boys," I said. "Someone who flies round the town in the night and goes down the chimneys and pulls the arms and legs off the boys and cooks them like sausages."

"Oh, shut up," Tom said.

I hit him, and he hit me back, and Rosie's mum said, "Stop it now. Please. All of you."

At once, Rosie set up a wail. "I didn't do anything."

"No, she didn't," I said. "It wasn't her fault. Just Tom and me fighting as usual."

"Oh, you two!" Rosie's mum said.

But she laughed. She didn't mind Tom and me fighting. She never said silly things like, "Boys don't hit girls." Or even, "Rosie doesn't fight, why can't you be more like her, Cat?"

Tom whispered to me, "If your granny's a Pag, you must be a Pag, too. She's a big Pag, you're a little Pag."

And we both rolled about, laughing. We were very young then, of course. Rosie and I were six, and Tom was seven.

It was a game between Tom and me for a long time. And a joke at school. When I was seven and eight, I growled as I ran after the little kids, pretending to be a

Pag-monster (only to tease, not to frighten), and if anyone was rude about my Pag-grandmother I thought of horrible things she might do to them, like locking them in a cage with savage rats, or putting them down in the sewer. It began to seem a bit silly by the time I was ten, but at least it took people's minds off my mother and father, who by this time were busy making fools of themselves on the telly, with parts in a new soap about an old people's home. (The Pag had bought me a television. I hardly ever watched it, except to find out what those two were up to.)

When we were eleven, Rosie and I went to the middle school. It was farther away than the primary, a boring journey by car over crowded roads but only four stations by tube. The other children in our class had chosen new schools closer to home, but Rosie's mum and the Pag had decided that this one would give us a better education, and that we were old enough to take the train on our own.

Tom had started at this school the year before. Although he made a huge fuss about having to travel with Rosie and me to begin with, he was really glad of our company. There was a long walk to the school from the tube station, up a hilly street (past Rosie and Tom's grandmother's house) and then along a path through a little wood and across a common. This was fine in the mornings, when it was light and people were walking their dogs, but going home in the afternoon, in the winter, it was a dark, scary walk for a person alone: trees rustling, and spooky shadows moving between them. Of course, Tom never said *he* was frightened, but when he and Rosie caught flu toward the end of the Christmas term, he told his mother he thought *I* might be. She told the Pag, and the Pag said she would come to fetch me.

She turned up on her bike. "Not worth getting the old car out just to stew in a traffic jam," she had said when I left in the morning, but somehow I hadn't expected to find her waiting at the school gate, looking like a person from outer space. For a minute it was as if this were the first time I had ever set eyes on her—on this strange creature, half-human, half-spider, gangly arms and legs in black leather, black helmet and goggles pushed back on her head, on top of what looked like a haystack rather than hair. And, of course, she was smoking.

I almost sneaked back into school. I could hide in the lavatories until most people had gone. Then no one would know she belonged to me. Somehow I would have to stop her coming tomorrow. I could say I'd met someone else who walked to the station. Or that I didn't mind the dark common . . .

But it was too late. She had seen me. She waved cheerfully. I managed to wave back, though my arms and legs felt stiff with horror and shame. Except for Rosie and

Tom, no one in this new school had ever seen the Pag. I knew they would have to see her eventually, but *not like this!* Not with the bike! Not in her leathers!

She said, "You've got a good high color, young Cat. School seems to suit you. Sling your stuff in the saddle-bag, put on your helmet, and we'll go for a real old zoom on the way home."

I couldn't speak. If I had been blushing before, I was like a furnace now. I got on the pillion, slammed on my helmet, and screwed up my eyes to pretend I was blind. I didn't want to know who was watching. Some of the people in my class were quite friendly, but they all were still sticking to their friends from their last school this first term, and Rosie and I were not certain yet who was nice, who was nasty. I had the feeling I was going to find out pretty soon, and as that thought came into my head, I couldn't help peeping. I saw several people from my class, standing and staring. Most of them just looked surprised. But one boy was grinning in a pleased, evil way. That was Willy. Horrible Willy. And I felt my heart turn cold in my chest and sink like a stone.

Chapter Three

I DIDN'T KNOW HIS SURNAME. Not until later. In the beginning he was just Willy who sat at the back of the class, flicking pellets of paper at people, and picking his nose, and flicking the pickings. Rosie and I called him Willy Snotnose. Not all the names we made up for people were so obvious, or so nasty, but Willy deserved it. He pinched, he sniggered, he sneered. He scrumpled up people's work if they left it on their desk for a minute. He stuck out his foot to trip the monitors up when they were carrying anything that might spill, like ink, or jugs of water at lunchtime. He never got into trouble because he made sure none of the teachers were looking or listening. And none of us told on him. We were not frightened, exactly. It just wasn't worth it. He could get his own back too easily.

Willy had a thin face and a long, thin nose, but his mouth was fat and droopy, the bottom lip hanging open to show the inside of his lip, wet and dark as a plum. Although he was skinny and not very tall, he had big, strong hands like a man's. I had seen him in the playground, sitting on top of a much bigger and older boy who was lying facedown and crying. Willy looked perfectly comfortable, grinning around at his gang as he held both the boy's wrists with one hand and picked his nose with the other.

There were three or four boys in his gang, none of them from our class, all of them bigger and older than he was. They met up at break and at lunchtime and stalked the playground like a pack of wolves looking for dinner. The sensible thing was not to look at them—or not to be caught looking, anyway. Rosie said, "If you look at them, that means you're insulting them, so it's okay to beat you up. If you don't look, that means you're invisible, so they don't see you. They want to hurt *someone*, but they need an excuse. It's a sort of game they play."

Rosie doesn't talk all that much. Not as much as I do, not as much as Tom. But when she does say something, you know she has worked it out properly. And she never seems to get into trouble. If she had been with me when Willy picked on me that day (the day after the Pag had come to school on the bike and embarrassed me), she would never have let me answer him back. She would have made me stalk off with my nose in the air!

But Rosie was at home, in bed with the flu. So I was playing with a girl called Fiona, who was my spare friend (like a spare tire) for when Rosie was busy. We were playing hopscotch—not very seriously, because we were growing out of this babyish game. And, suddenly, Willy Snotnose was there, leaning against the wall, picking his nose and grinning.

I refused to look at him. He sniggered slyly, to attract my attention, and I just tossed my hair back and hopped more energetically. Then he said, "I say, Cat, who's the old witch you went off with last night?"

I gave him a withering look.

He said, "I was just asking a *question*! I mean, she's a bit old to be anyone's mother."

I said nothing. Fiona said, "I've got to go somewhere." And ran off toward the girls' lavatories.

Willy said, in a different tone of voice, "That's an excellent bike she's got. Whoever she is. I mean, it's a real biker's bike."

"It's a Harley-Davidson," I said. "She used to have a Vincent Black Shadow but that's in a museum now."

I had been taken in because he had sounded simply interested, not sarcastic or spiteful. But as soon as I had spoken I knew it had been a mistake. I had fallen into his trap, made myself *visible*.

He said, "Where's the coven, Cat? Do you dance

around a fire with your clothes off? Can I come and watch sometime? I promise I won't tell anyone."

His fat droopy mouth was wetter than ever. I said, "You're *disgusting*. Willy Wet-Mouth. Willy Snotnose. Did you know that's what everyone calls you?"

His pale eyes sparked bright as if a light had been turned on behind them. He came close to me and I could see myself in them. I stepped back, but I was determined not to turn tail and run. I said, "You touch me, Snotnose, I'll kill you."

I knew I wouldn't have a chance. But I was so angry I didn't care. And, in fact, all he did was catch hold of my wrist and twist the skin in a quick burn. I thumped him with my free hand and he let me go. He laughed in his sneery way and said, "That's just a free sample."

The Light of Science appeared in the playground, clanging the bell for afternoon school. (She was the English teacher, in fact, but Rosie had chosen that name for her out of the hymn that begins "These things shall be, a loftier race" because she was about seven feet tall.)

I turned my back on Willy and set off as quickly as I could without running. He was just behind me, and when I had to slow down because we were all bunched up, trying to get through the door of the classroom, I could feel his breath on my neck. He said in my ear, "That's why you're called Cat, isn't it? You've got that black hair. Witches always have black cats. Will she come to fetch you from school on her broomstick?"

I began to be really scared then. I had persuaded the Pag that I would be quite all right today, coming home on my own. "Tom's a fusspot, Pag, honestly. It's *him* hates the dark on the common, not me. And some of the bigger girls go that way to the station, I can always tag along with them." And because the Pag had been too busy to listen properly (she was going to London to give one of her lectures at the university), she had believed me.

We had two lessons that afternoon, English with the Light of Science and French with the Tooth Fairy. I didn't hear a word either of them said. I couldn't make up my mind whether it would be better to get out of school *fast* before Willy had collected his gang or to hang about, hide until they had given me up and gone home. I thought, *If I had Rosie's grandmother's telephone number, I could ring and ask her to come and meet me halfway on the common,* though if I did that, Rosie's grandmother would tell Rosie's mother and Rosie's mother would tell the Pag, who would know I had lied to her. And, anyway, I didn't have Rosie's grandmother's telephone number.

In the end I decided on running. I was out of the gate, coat buttoned up wrong, shoelaces flapping, within minutes of slamming my desk shut. I am quite a good runner (a good swimmer, too, though no good at ball games) and I was over the common and through the wood at a speed that astonished me. I looked back, and there was no one behind me. I wondered if I should go and see Rosie's grandmother, but I wasn't sure if she would want to see me without Rosie and Tom, and so I ran on to the station.

I had forgotten there were fewer trains at this time of day, before the evening rush hour when the shops and offices closed, and that one of the reasons we stopped to see Rosie's grandmother after school was because otherwise we had a long wait on a cold, empty platform. When I got to the station there was no one about except the man in the ticket office, and once I had gone through the barrier and across the bridge and down the stairs to the tracks, there was no one at all. It had begun to be foggy; the lights in the station were fuzzy and dim and there seemed to be more shadows than usual. There was a waiting room with *Ladies* painted in yellow paint on the door, but there was no light inside, and no lock.

There was no place to hide, so I stood under the stairs and hoped the train would come soon. I counted under my breath. I thought, *If I get to a thousand and nothing happens, I'll get safely home.*

I had got to six hundred and nineteen when I heard the train shaking the rails. At the same time, someone was coming down the wooden steps above my head. Slow, thumping treads, like an old, heavy person. And a quicker, pattering sound. I shrank against the greasy wall under the stairs. Even if Willy hadn't followed me over the common, he knew that Rosie and I took the train home.

But it was only a blind man with his dog. The train drew up with a hissing of brakes, the doors opened, the man got into the last carriage, and I followed him. As far as I had been able to tell, peering in as it rattled past, the rest of the train was empty. *Better a blind man than no one,* I thought. I cleared my throat and said "Good girl" to the dog, so her master should know I was there.

He moved his head in my direction but that was all. He wore very dark glasses and I had an uncomfortable feeling that in spite of the dog and the white stick, he was watching me.

I waited for the train to move. I said to the blind man, "Do you think the train's stuck in this station?"—giving a bit of a laugh, making a joke of it. But he said nothing, just sat there, his blank, white, doughy face turned toward me.

The train gave a little lurch. I said, in the same bright, sociable way, "Well, it seems to have made up its mind to do *something*," and at that very moment they came tearing down the steps to the platform, whooping and screaming, and flung themselves into the carriage. The doors closed behind them and they collapsed on the seats, on the same side as the blind man and opposite me.

There were only three of them. Willy Snotnose, Fat Boy, and Fish Breath. Fish Breath was the oldest, fourteen or fifteen, Rosie and I had decided, when we had first marked him down as one of the gang. Fat Boy was in

Tom's class, so at the time this happened he would have been twelve, just a year older than me. I sat, staring at them and thinking how *ugly* the three of them were. Fish Breath especially, with his bulgy eyes like golf balls and a mouth full of what looked like black, rotting spikes. I thought I might ask Rosie if she reckoned being so ugly had brought them together. And then I asked myself if I would live to see Rosie again.

I didn't really believe they would kill me. Thinking this was what the Pag calls gallows humor, which is making a joke to keep your spirits up when bad things are happening. And it did make me feel braver. After their noisy rush into the carriage they had gone quiet and were staring at me without any expression, all three of them. I thought, *That's all they are going to do! Try to frighten me!*

Fish Breath said, in a quiet, dangerous voice, "Willy don't like being called rude, nasty names."

The blind man moved his head in Fish Breath's direction but gave no other sign of having heard.

Willy said, "Witch's Cat. Dirty old witch's black cat. How d'you like it?"

I said, "There's no such thing as witches. You know that perfectly well. Witches are for children's stories, not for real life."

Fat Boy started rolling round in his seat, hooting with laughter. In between hoots, he said, "Tell her, Willy. Tell her what you're going to do to her." His fat face was shining. I tried to think what he looked like so I could tell Rosie. But all I could think was that he looked hungry.

The blind man stood up. The dog's harness jangled softly as she led him to the other end of the carriage. He sat down with his back to us.

Fish Breath said softly, "See? He don't want to get caught up in anything."

I felt sick. The blind man must know that something was wrong. Perhaps he couldn't do much to help me. But he was a grown man! And he had turned his back on me.

He got out at the next station. There were people waiting on the platform, but when the doors opened there was no one close to our carriage. And Willy jumped on me at once. When the doors had closed, he wrapped my hair round his hand, so tight that I thought he would tear it out by the roots. I said, "That man got off the train to fetch the police. They'll catch you at the next station." But I didn't believe it.

Willy gave my hair a tug that seemed to tear my scalp off. I said, "If you hurt me, if you do *anything* to me, you'll be in really bad trouble. My granny isn't a witch, but she *is* a Pag! Bet you don't know what that is!"

"Stupid brat," Fish Breath said. "Shall I light her up, Willy?"

He had a cigarette lighter in his hand. The yellow flame shot out several inches. He said, "If she's a witch, it won't burn her."

I screamed then. Screamed and screamed. But the train was rattling and banging through the dark tunnel. I shut my eyes and threw myself about and I thought I smelt a singeing smell, my hair burning. Willy said, "Shut up, you silly cow."

I opened my eyes then and saw his pale eyes and wet mouth close to mine. He had let go my hair and was holding my arms spread out either side of me, forced back, hurting my shoulders. He was kneeling on the bench seat, pinning my legs down with his. I could see Fat Boy and Fish Breath beyond him, leering at me over his shoulders. I thought, *Suppose one of them has a knife!*

I felt calm suddenly. I knew what to do—the only thing I *could* do.

I said, "Don't you know about Pags? They aren't witches, of course, But they are special people. I shouldn't be telling you this. It's a secret. But if you let me go, then I'll tell you."

I looked straight into Willy's pale eyes. I wasn't afraid—I told myself I wasn't afraid. And he was the one who blinked first. He didn't let go my arms altogether but he loosened his grip.

I said, speaking very slowly and in the most secretive and thrilling voice I could manage, "They are the people who have all the power in the world. Not just prime ministers and presidents, but astronauts and spies and great scientists. The sort of people who make all the really important things happen. You don't always know who they are, even if they live next door to you, that's the most secret thing. But *they* know, and if you hurt one of them, or hurt someone who belongs to their family, the others will get you. . . ."

The train was out of the tunnel now, rushing through the next station without stopping, as it often did in the afternoons, and into the black tunnel again. Only about another two and a half minutes, unless the train stopped in the tunnel. That happened sometimes because the electric cables were about a hundred years old and needed repairing. I thought Willy was looking puzzled. As if he didn't know what to do next.

Fat Boy said, "Shut the stupid brat up." (He said something much ruder than *stupid brat,* but I don't care to write it.) Then, "Your dad's a Pag, come to that, Willy."

Willy had stopped kneeling over me. There were pins and needles in my legs. My arms were free, too, but I didn't dare stretch them or rub them in case Willy hadn't realized he had let me go.

The train was slowing down. My station was a busy one because it was near a big shopping center, and as soon as the doors opened, about twenty women and several hundred yellow plastic bags filled up the carriage.

I had to push my way out. None of the gang tried to stop me, but halfway up the stairs to the footbridge I looked over my shoulder and saw them at the bottom—

not Fish Breath but Fat Boy, his face bobbing like a red balloon, and Willy. He was shouting something.

People were running down the stairs in a hurry to catch the train, which was still at the platform. A man said, "Look where you're going, young lady." Then I heard the dogs barking.

The Pag was waiting on the far side of the footbridge, with Sally and Amber and Wilkins-the-Mongrel. She was wearing her black wool and the Brooch. She had put her hair up on top of her head, as she usually did when she was giving a lecture. It made her seem taller than ever, proud-looking and fierce. Not weird at all, I thought suddenly; more like a queen, or a duchess.

She said, "I got back in time, so I thought, might as well give some of the old dogs a run." Then she looked at me properly. "What's the matter, what's wrong, Catikin?"

She didn't often call me a pet name. It brought tears into my throat. I turned and pointed at Willy, who was on the footbridge behind me. There was no sign of Fat Boy. I said, "They chased me on the train. Him and the others. They *teased* me."

It had been much worse than teasing. But it was the only word I could think of just at that moment. And the dogs were jumping up, whimpering, and trying to lick me. Now I was safe, I was afraid of making a fuss about nothing. Especially when Willy came up, holding out my school bag. He said, "You left this behind, Cat."

It was a different boy who smiled at the Pag, not the Willy who had pinned me down in the carriage. This Willy's gray eyes danced merrily either side of his bony nose, and the smile stopped his lower lip hanging loose and made his fat mouth look gentle. He said to the Pag, "I thought she might need it for homework."

I said, "They were going to burn me. To set fire to my hair."

"It wasn't me," Willy said. "And it was only a joke. But he shouldn't have done it." He was still holding my bag.

I took it from him. The Pag said, "Cat?" and I growled a thank you.

"That's all right, it's no trouble," Willy said. He put out his hand to pat the nearest dog, Wilkins-the-Mongrel, and snatched it back quickly as Wilkins lifted his lip in a snarl.

The Pag looked from Willy to me and back to Willy again. She said, "I don't know what has happened, and if Cat doesn't tell me I won't try to guess. But I tell you one thing, young man. If you bully my granddaughter, I will not only inform the authorities, your parents, and your teachers, but I will myself, personally, throw you *so hard* into the middle of next week that you may never come back."

Written down, this looks more of a joke than a threat. But the way the Pag said it, with pure, ice-cold menace, as if it really meant something, sent shivers down my spine.

And it drained the blood from Willy's face so that for the first time in my life I saw what people meant when they said "white as a sheet."

He turned and ran. The Pag frowned to herself and muttered something under her breath. I said, "What?" and she shook her head, meaning it wasn't important, or if it *was* important she wasn't going to tell me.

She said "Heel" to the dogs. Then she took my hand, which was something she hadn't done for years, not since I had learned to cross busy roads by myself, and held it tight all the way home.

Chapter Four

WILLY WASN'T AT SCHOOL the next day, which was a relief in one way and not in another. I needed to know what he was going to do, to find out and get it over and done with.

Luckily, Rosie and Tom were well enough to come to school with me. Rosie would never be much use in a fight but she has a quick, sharp tongue and sometimes, with boys, that works better. In the train, I told Tom about Fat Boy because they were in the same class, and Tom said not to worry.

Tom said, "He only ever goes after the little kids. I'll just tell him, he bullies you and I'll sort him out. He'll be sorry!"

Although Tom sounded so boastful, he was looking awful after his flu, red around the eyes and still coughing. I said he wasn't to get in a fight for my sake and he said, suddenly angry, "Don't nag at me, you're not my mother," and refused to speak to me for the rest of the journey.

Willy wasn't there for assembly, nor for the first couple of lessons. I decided that he had been given permission to miss part of morning school because he had to go to the dentist, and when the classroom door finally opened, my stomach gave a lurch, as if I were going up in a lift or an airplane. But it wasn't Willy coming in late after a dentist appointment. It was the school secretary, to say that the headmaster would like to see Catriona Brooke in his office.

As I followed her down the corridor, trying to keep up with the click-clack of her high black heels, I thought of reasons why Hairy Ears should have sent for me, starting with the absolute worst, which was that the Pag had fallen off her bike and was all broken up in the hospital, then running through obvious things like being given a million pounds by a shaky old man I had helped cross the road and who had tracked me to the school by my uniform, and ending with good, cheerful reasons like my odious parents leaving the country forever. (That was just fanciful. If my mother and father were doing a moonlight flit, they wouldn't bother to inform Hairy Ears. Or even the Pag, come to that!)

As we reached the headmaster's office the door opened and a man marched out, looking angry. He was in such a hurry that he collided with the school secretary. Although he apologized to her, he looked as if he would have liked to knock her down and tread on her face. As for me, I was no more than a fly or a cockroach, to be swept aside or murdered with bug spray, whichever came easier.

He was a tall man with a thin, foxy face. He reminded me of someone but I didn't have time to think who it might be because the secretary had tapped on the headmaster's door and was standing aside to usher me in.

Hairy Ears has no hair on his head; no hair at all, not even the most delicate wisp. And his face is round and pink and smooth as a baby's. All his hairy genes are concentrated in his big, floppy ears, where the hair grows long and thick and tufty, so that he looks as if he has two stiff brushes growing out of the sides of his face.

When we first came to this school, Rosie and I couldn't look at Hairy Ears without laughing. But by now, toward the end of my first term, he had begun to seem—well, not normal *exactly*, but certainly less of a freak.

Today, for example, I barely noticed his ears. He was smiling at me, but it was a worried sort of a smile and I began to be afraid. Perhaps the Pag really had had an accident. Perhaps my thinking about it had made it happen!

Hairy Ears said, "Sit down, Catriona. I'm sorry to take you out of your class, but I want to talk to you about William Green."

Who was William Green?

Hairy Ears said, "He's in your form, Catriona. Perhaps you know him as Willy? Or Bill?"

That was who the foxy-faced, angry man had reminded me of. I said, "Willy. That's what we all call him. I didn't know his name was Green."

Hairy Ears said, "His father has just been to see me. He's one of our school governors. Sir Archibald Wellington Plunkett Green."

I said nothing. There was nothing to say. I hoped I looked thoughtful and intelligent.

Hairy Ears said, "Sir Archibald told me that William and two of his friends were on the train with you yesterday and there was some trouble between you. Of course, he has only heard his son's story. I would like to hear yours, Catriona."

I couldn't think what he meant. I was dumb.

Hairy Ears said, "If you would prefer to discuss this with Mrs. Morgan, I can ask her to speak to you in the lunch hour."

Mrs. Morgan was the one Rosie and I called the Light of Science. I thought gratefully, *At least I know who she is!* She was our form mistress as well as our English teacher.

I said, "I don't know what Willy said, do I? They chased me onto the train. Willy's gang."

"And they teased you, is that it? Why do you think they picked on you, Catriona?"

I said, "I don't know. They just do that, those boys."

"Had you been calling them names?"

He sounded interested, not angry. I said, "They weren't just teasing me. Teasing's the wrong word for what they were doing. Teasing doesn't sound serious. They tried to burn my hair with a cigarette lighter."

Hairy Ears said, very gently, as if he didn't want to upset me, "What sort of names did you call them?"

How could I tell him? *Snotnose! Fish Breath!*

Hairy Ears said, "Names can hurt, Catriona. Particularly when people are young and not very sure of themselves."

I nodded. I was being put in the wrong. But I couldn't see what to do about it.

Hairy Ears sighed. He said, "Apparently Willy is very upset. He is a sensitive boy, so his father says. Can you remember, Catriona, exactly what happened when you got off the train?"

"Willy ran after me." I added, without thinking, "So did Fat Boy."

"I see." Hairy Ears had taken a pencil out of the jar on his desk and was drawing squiggles on a sheet of paper. Then he threw the pencil down and looked at me. "We will forget about Fat Boy for the moment. Except to say that you are quite old enough to know it is cruel to mock people for physical attributes that they may be sensitive about."

I thought, *Hairy Ears should know all about that!* I stared at his shiny bald head and he ran his hand over it, a bit nervously, as if he had guessed what I was thinking. I said, "Everyone calls him Fat Boy, it isn't just me."

"Was it you who called Willy *Snotnose?*" he asked suddenly, and I couldn't help giggling; it was so funny to hear Hairy Ears say this rude name aloud, and in such a shocked, solemn voice.

I looked at my lap. I had called our French teacher the Tooth Fairy because she had sparkly false teeth that flashed when she laughed, but it was Rosie who had made up all the other names. The really unkind names. And I couldn't give Rosie away.

Hairy Ears sighed. He said, "Why did Willy run after you when you got off the train? His father says it was because you forgot your school bag."

I muttered, "That's what Willy *said*. He might have just been pretending in front of my grandmother."

"Ah!" Hairy Ears said. "Yes. Your grandmother." He looked into the space behind my head. I could hear the clock ticking on the wall. It was a plump sound. Hairy Ears said, "Your grandmother frightened William, it seems. Threatened him, so Sir Archibald says."

I didn't know what to say. It seemed silly to tell him

what the Pag had said to Willy. Saying you were going to knock someone into the middle of next week was a joke, even when it didn't sound like a joke. I said, "She just told him to stop bullying me."

Hairy Ears said, "When William got off the train with your bag, he didn't know your grandmother was meeting you, did he? Don't you think it is possible, Catriona, that he might have been sorry? That running after you to give you your bag was a kind of apology?"

If Hairy Ears believed that, he'd believe anything! And he wanted me to agree with him. To say *I* was sorry. That Willy Snotnose was really a nice, kind, good boy. That was a kind of bullying, too. Not as bad as trying to set fire to someone, but horrible all the same because I couldn't answer back.

I could have told him what the Pag sometimes said when people gave nice reasons for bad behavior instead of the true, nasty ones: "Lay not that flattering unction to thy soul." But I didn't dare say this to Hairy Ears. Even though it was a quotation from Shakespeare.

So I said, "I don't know, do I? I mean, how could I know? You'd have to be inside Willy's *mind* to know for sure, wouldn't you?"

Hairy Ears looked at me. I could hear the clock ticking again. It must have been ticking all the time we were talking. I thought, *It's quite loud, why couldn't I hear it?*

Hairy Ears said, "Catriona, why are you so angry?"

38

That took me by surprise. I burst out, "You saying it's all my fault. I mean, that's not fair. You weren't there. It's just because Willy's *father* came and complained about me and he's a school governor. I'm sorry if he was upset, Willy's father. But he shouldn't say things he doesn't know. He wasn't there, either."

There was a long silence. At least, it seemed long to me, and I began to feel a bit frightened. But Hairy Ears was looking at me with a strange, sad expression.

He cleared his throat suddenly. He picked up the pencil he had thrown down on the desk and waggled it between his fingers.

He said, watching the pencil, not looking at me, "You must feel that William Green is lucky to have a dad around to stand up for him. I can sympathize with that, Catriona. It's not easy for you, with your mother and father always away and your grandmother—well, of course, I know she is very distinguished, but she is a very old lady to be bringing up a young girl. I explained your circumstances to Sir Archibald and I think he was disposed to be understanding. . . ."

I said, "He didn't look understanding. He looked *mad*."

"Don't be pert, Catriona."

Hairy Ears was annoyed because I had interrupted him. But this wasn't the first time I'd had to put up with grownups pitying me for my unnatural home life. The PE teacher had kept me behind one day after netball to ask me if my grandmother had talked to me about starting my periods. As if at the Pag's great age she might have forgotten! And after that, a dietician came, doing a survey about what schoolchildren ate for breakfast. Our class was asked, each person in turn, and I said I'd just had some of the dogs' rusks for breakfast. The dog rusks were stale wholemeal bread baked in the oven, and I liked them with lots of butter and honey or dripping with soft-boiled egg yolk, much better than fresh bread or toast. But Mrs. Morgan gave me a funny look and the next week she set us an essay for homework on My Favorite Food, which had to be about what we actually ate as well as what we would like to eat. Rosie, who has a delicate stomach, said it was all my fault for giving the Light of Science the idea that the Pag fed me on scraps.

Hairy Ears said, "William is going into hospital for surgery, for an operation on his sinuses. He is not returning to school until after Christmas. Perhaps, in that time, you could try to forget the cruel name you called him and make up your mind to treat him more kindly next term. And if you have any trouble from the other two boys who were involved in this unfortunate incident, you will tell Mrs. Morgan or come straight to me, and we will deal with them. Is that understood, Catriona?"

I was seething inside, But I stood up straight as a poker and kept my face solid and still as I said, "Yes, sir. I understand, sir."

Tom beat up Fat Boy three days later. He got knocked about himself, too, so his form teacher, a skinny old man called Muckleberry whom Rosie hadn't thought of a name for because his own was funny enough, only gave them both a black mark for fighting in the playground and sent them to the washroom to clean themselves up. Fish Breath kept his distance. I saw him once or twice but as soon as he saw me he just melted away. "It isn't a gang without Willy," Rosie said. "Any luck, they won't get together again when he comes back. Things sort of wear out. Just don't *look*, Cat. It was you *looking* started the trouble."

✧

Christmas came. The Pag got two medical students to house-sit and look after the animals, and she and I went to Greece, to the old house in a mountain village she bought years and years ago and has promised to leave to me when she dies. It hasn't got central heating, but the walls are stone and four feet thick, and once the fire has been lit the whole place warms up and stays warm. We didn't have a Christmas tree because the Pag says the Greeks need their trees in the ground, not dug up and then thrown away like useless clutter, but she gave me a fat book of Greek myths and a beautiful black velvet miniskirt and a white cashmere sweater, and I gave her a book of poems about cats and a five-year

41

diary bound in red leather, to make sure she stayed alive until I was at least seventeen. We went for long walks on the mountain, and ate at the taverna, and played bezique by the fire.

One evening, after supper, I thought I might tell her about Hairy Ears and what he had said about Willy. I started by saying, "You remember that horrible boy you told off that time at the station?" I wanted to tell her that I kept hearing him saying sneering things in my head. But although I hoped she would laugh and tell me not to be silly, I was afraid she might be hurt underneath.

So I wasn't too sorry when she just nodded absently, looking into the fire, as if she had half heard me but was too busy thinking hard about something else to answer me at the moment. Or perhaps she hadn't heard me at all. The wind was booming around the cottage. And she was a bit deaf.

Then she said suddenly, "Would you rather have stayed at home, Cat? At your age, at Christmas, you should be with your friends. Having fun. Going to parties. Not stuck halfway up a freezing Greek mountain with an old bag like me."

I said, "You're a Pag. Not a Bag. Not even a Hag."

But she didn't laugh. She was *serious*.

I said, "I'm not sure I'm exactly ready for Acid House Raves. And I don't have all that many friends except Rosie and Tom. I mean, friends I *want* to be with."

She sighed. She lit one of her smelly cigarettes and wrinkled her eyes against the smoke. She still wasn't looking at me.

I said, "Most people I know would give a lot to have a house in Greece to go to, with the sea and the sun and the swimming."

She said in her hoarse, smoky voice, "I suppose it's all right in the summer."

I said, "What's *wrong* with you? Something you ate?"

She didn't smile. She didn't answer.

I said, "I *love* being here, just you and me, don't you know that?"

This wasn't quite true. I liked being with the Pag, just the two of us, but the only advantage to Greece in the winter was that none of her mad old patients could get hold of her, either telephone or turn up, which they were liable to do at holiday times when they felt especially lonely. Last year, at Christmas, old Flossie had arrived on the doorstep at lunchtime, dressed in what might have been, a very long time ago, someone else's cast-off party clothes. She was wearing a pink satin blouse and a short, tight, satin skirt that showed her soft, bulgy, white knees, black socks wrinkled round her ankles, and an old pair of running shoes. She hadn't washed before she put on this festive attire and the whiff from her armpits rather spoiled the lovely smell of the goose, but when she left she said "Thank you for having me" quite politely and actually smiled, which astonished me. After she'd gone, I said to the Pag, "Must be the first time anyone's seen the inside of Flossie's mouth for years. I don't suppose she goes to the dentist that often!"

The Pag has quite a taste for silly jokes usually. It's one of the un-grown-up things about her that make her fun to be with. She did smile, but quickly, turning away, and not before I had seen tears in her eyes. And although I knew why—Flossie dressed up for a party was a pitiful sight as well as a funny one—this was the first time I had seen the Pag cry, and it made me feel shaky.

It struck me now that she might have decided to come to Greece for Christmas just to avoid old Flossie, or Mr. Wilberforce Frisbee, or any other unwelcome but impossible-to-turn-away visitor turning up for Christmas dinner. She didn't mind for herself. But she thought her funny old people were boring for me.

I said, "I didn't mean it wasn't nice when Flossie came last year. I mean, I enjoyed that, too, making her happy."

The Pag looked at me then. Her expression was sad. She said, "You should have gone to your mother and father this Christmas."

She always said "your mother," I realized suddenly. Never "my daughter."

I laughed. I said, "No way! *No way*, not *ever*. You know that, don't you? For one thing, there's no room in that horrible flat. The last time I went I had to sleep on the floor, in a sort of closet without any windows. And they don't *want* me there, anyway."

"Whether they do or don't, the fact is they asked you." The Pag sat up, very straight-backed and brisk suddenly. "To be exact, your mother told me to *tell* you. They've bought a house. Settling down at last, is what your mother said. So of course they want you to live with them."

I couldn't believe what I was hearing. Nor could I tell what the Pag was thinking. Her eyes were unblinking, still as blue ice.

I said, "I won't go! You know I won't, don't you? You can't *make* me. I'd run away. . . ."

Then I thought, *That's just what the Pag's done, of course.* She hadn't told me we were going to Greece until the day before Christmas Eve. I thought she'd kept it till then as a surprise; instead, she had booked our flights at the very last minute so that we could escape from my mother. *Her daughter!*

I got up and ran at her, stumbling. She opened her arms and held me tight on her bony lap. I said into her shoulder, "*We've* run away, haven't we? I wondered why you made up your mind all of a sudden."

She rocked me backward and forward. I was so relieved! I was snuffling, half crying, half laughing. I said, "I knew you'd never send me away."

She made a funny noise deep in her throat. She pushed me away from her and I slid off her lap and knelt at her feet. Then she put her long, twiggy hands either side of my face and stroked my chin with her thumbs. Her fingers were rough but she meant to be loving and so I kept still.

She said, "I told your mother she would have to be patient. I told her she must give us both time to get used to it."

Chapter Five

WE ARGUED ABOUT IT in Greece. We argued about it in the plane flying to London. We argued about it at home.

The Pag said, "I'm sure, when she thinks about it, your mother will want to do what is best for you. I think she was just so pleased with the new house, she wanted you to see it at once. She has always been impatient. But you are impatient, too, aren't you, Cat?"

The Pag said, "Of course she loves you. Your mother and father both love you. But it's difficult for actors to look after children, especially in the live theater. Out every night, and often on tour round the country. It's easier now they are both working for the same television company. They can rehearse and record the installments in the daytime and be home in the evenings."

The Pag said, "I know they forgot your birthday last year."

The Pag said, "I know the blue sweater they sent you last Christmas was two sizes too small."

The Pag said, "You have to give people a chance, Catriona."

I said, "Don't you dare call me Catriona."

I said, "It wasn't just last year."

I said, "Why are you sticking up for them all of a sudden?"

I said, "You want to get rid of me, don't you?"

I said, "All right, then, you *don't* want to get rid of me. That just makes you a slimy, horrible *traitor*."

In the end I said I would go for a week at half-term. Only for a week, and only to see how I liked it. I would go by train and come back by train. *On my own.* I couldn't stop my mother or father telephoning the Pag secretly, but I didn't want them all getting together, *in person*, plotting against me. A week would be quite long enough for my mother and father. I would be such a brat, they would be glad to be rid of me.

"They'll be sorry," I said to the Pag.

She didn't answer. She had tried appealing to my better nature. Now she was going in for low cunning. There were these pointed silences. I was being so childish, they said, no sensible grownup would argue the point with me. And she asked me to help her sort out the old photographs she kept in a muddly drawer of her desk in the dining room. She knew I loved looking at the family pictures she had brought with her from Poland, even though they were faded and brown and turning up at the edges. But although she had always enjoyed telling me tales about my long-ago ancestors, that wasn't what she was after this time!

There were a few photographs of my mother as a fat baby, sitting in a pram like an ordinary infant, but most of them showed her, at various stages of growth, pretending to be something else. She was dressed as a butterfly, as a snowflake, as a Japanese doll in a kimono with a broad sash round her small, solid waist. In other pictures she was wearing long, silky dresses that belonged to a grownup and high-heeled shoes miles too big for her.

The Pag said, "Your mother was an actress from the very beginning. Look at her in that old dress of mine and those shoes. You'd never believe she was only four!"

I looked at the Pag, not at the picture. I said, "Those can't be your clothes she's wearing! I *do not believe it!* You've *never* worn heels like that in your life!"

"It was a long time ago," the Pag said.

She picked out a photograph of my mother aged about eight or nine, in a white nightie with a blue handkerchief tied round her head. She was supposed to be the Virgin Mary. Joseph was standing behind her and there was a wicker cradle in front of them with a doll in it. Joseph was looking cross, but my mother was simpering at the camera in a repulsively soppy way, as if she was expecting everyone to clap their hands and cry, "Isn't she sweet!"

I said, "Yuck!"

The Pag shuffled the photographs hastily. In the next horror, my mother was about ten or eleven, wearing a hideous dress covered in frills from neck to hem, long white socks, and black patent shoes.

The Pag said, "She looks a bit like you, don't you think, Cat? Something about the eyes . . ."

I groaned. "Don't be pathetic! Who's she dressed up as this time?"

The Pag laughed, pretending to believe this was such a silly question it was hardly worth answering. "She's wearing her own party frock. She was going to a party."

"Oh," I said. "Pardon *me*! I would never have guessed it! I thought she must be going off to play football!"

With the Pag going in for all this propaganda that was

meant to make me love my mother, there was no time to talk to her about Hairy Ears and Willy Snotnose. And in fact they had grown a bit dim in my mind—faded and faraway like the old photographs the Pag had brought from Poland all those years ago. So I was quite surprised when she said, the first morning of term, just as I was going out through the door, "If that boy—whatsis-name?—makes a nuisance of himself, mind you tell me."

To anyone who didn't know her, this might have sounded like something that had only popped into her mind at that minute and would pop out again just as quickly. But the Pag hardly ever said anything she hadn't thought about beforehand. She was a little like Rosie in that way. If the Pag had sounded casual just now, it was because she didn't want me to think she was worrying.

So I said, "Oh, *him*! Silly old Willy! At least, I *think* that's his name. I'd forgotten about him. I don't suppose he'll be any trouble."

It was a bright, frosty morning, the kind of morning when there is crackly ice on the puddles and your ears sing with the cold. Rosie and Tom and I set off early; I had only come back from Greece two days before and we had a lot of talk to catch up on—what we'd done in the holidays, that sort of thing. I won't set it down because it had nothing to do with what happened later. (You have to make up your mind what to leave out when you're writing a story. If you put everything in about one particular morning, what clothes you put on, how long you took cleaning your teeth, what you ate for breakfast, and what you said to your grandmother, the story would be as long as your life and no one would have time to read it.)

Instead, I will describe Rosie and Tom, which is something I haven't done up to now. Rosie is taller than I am and much prettier. She has brown eyes with long lashes and beautiful, frizzy, gold-and-brown hair. She is quite solemn-looking, as if she often finds life a bit of a puzzle. Tom is about the same height as Rosie, even though he is older, but his mother says he will be as tall as his dad. She says she can tell by the size of his feet, which are huge. In the meantime they just make him look fairly ridiculous. Like a stick insect in boots. But Tom doesn't get tormented for his appearance. Not because he is sharp-tongued, like Rosie, or even because he's a good fighter, but because most people like him too much to be nasty. When he gets angry, it's never for long, and the minute he stops, he gives one of his enormous grins, almost splitting his face in two, laughing at himself for losing his temper and making everyone else laugh along with him.

We were crossing the common when I started thinking about Willy Snotnose and how I would most probably be seeing him in assembly in about twenty minutes. I wasn't exactly looking forward to it but I wasn't scared either. I said—*muttered*, really, talking under my breath to myself, thinking aloud—something about Willy, how I hoped he wasn't going to make trouble for me this term.

I don't know what I expected either of them to say. All I know is that I was *flabbergasted*, bowled over, and just about *stamped flat* by Rosie's answer.

She said, "If you went to live with your mother and father you'd have to go to another school, and then Willy couldn't bully you any longer."

It might have been all right for me to say something like that as a sort of joke, the Pag's gallows humor, but it was all wrong for Rosie. If Tom had said it I would have thumped him. But if I thumped Rosie, she would just act the martyr. So in spite of boiling inside, I said, in a sorrowful voice, "You sound as if you'd be pleased! I thought you were my friend!"

Tom said, "Don't be feeble-minded, Cat. You know Rosie didn't mean that!"

I thought of something else. I said, "How'd you know, anyway?"

As soon as I had spoken I knew the answer. The day we got home from Greece, their mother had come round with a casserole for our supper, which was something she often did; she liked cooking, she said, and it was never any trouble to make a bit extra. I would have stayed home if I'd known she was coming, I liked Rosie's mum, but as she came up the path I was just setting off for a walk with three of the dogs, to make up for being away over Christmas. (The fourth dog, the old pug called Boot, was too stiff in the joints to go out any longer.) And so there was plenty of time for the Pag to tell Rosie's mother about the wicked plans *my* mother had thought up for me!

I said bitterly, "I suppose your mother thinks I ought to go and live with my parents. I suppose *you* think I ought to! I suppose you've all talked it over together."

There was a painful lump in my throat, hard as a stone. I started to walk fast, so fast my cheeks jolted. I said over my shoulder, "We're going to be late if we don't hurry," and started to run.

I knew Rosie couldn't catch me, she was no good at running, and Tom was weighed down with a lot of extra kit, a bulging satchel and a long, sausage-shaped tote bag. He could never make up his mind what he was going to need, and so he always brought everything that might come in useful, like his old rugger boots as well as his new ones, the book he was going to read when he finished the one he was reading, his set of wrenches in case someone needed a wrench, his super glue, a tube of glue remover, plus anything else that was special to him at the moment. The Pag and I had brought him a little bronze horse from Athens, a beautiful copy of the real one in the museum, and he had been playing with it on the train, stroking and feeling it.

In spite of his heavy load, he was at my heels as I wheeled into the playground.

"My lungs are *bursting*," he complained. He was snorting and grunting as if he might really drop dead any minute. I stopped running and said, "Okay, *okay*, I don't want your death on my hands!"

He staggered about for a bit, clutching at the air, acting the fool, until I couldn't help laughing. Then he said, "Look, you just *tell* me. I'll see to him. I'm older than he is."

But not as strong, I thought, *not as nasty*. Besides, it wasn't just Willy. There was Fat Boy. And Fish Breath.

Rosie came up beside me. Her face was flushed. She said, "I was only just *thinking*, Cat."

Although she sounded reproachful—anything she had *thought* about was okay to *say*, in Rosie's view—I knew she was sorry. I tried to explain. I said, "Your saying that, it was like telling me to chop my foot off because I've got a blister. I mean, it's too *drastic*. Anyway, I'm not scared of Willy!"

And I wasn't—or not at that precise moment. It was walking into the classroom a bit later on that I began to feel jumpy. He was already there, rummaging in his desk on the other side of the room. I had time to notice that he was taller and thinner and that his long, bony nose had grown even longer and bonier. Then he looked up and saw me, and I felt suddenly dizzy.

He didn't *do* anything. For what felt like ages, he stood quite still and stared at me with shiny gray eyes that seemed much paler and rounder than I remembered. Then he smiled. Not a nice smile, but not an absolutely nasty smile, either. Just the kind of sly smirk that says, *I know something you don't know and I'm not telling you.* And when he had made me feel really uncomfortable he looked away and went back to his rummaging. (I was fairly sure he wasn't looking for anything in particular, just trying to show he was far too important and busy to pay attention to me!)

Apart from giving me that look, the *I know something* look, whenever he looked at me and caught me looking at him, nothing happened. Not that first day, nor the next, nor all that week, nor the week after, nor the week after that.

Nothing happened.

Nothing happened.

NOTHING HAPPENED.

NOTHING . . . HAPPENED.

Chapter Six

YOU'D THINK I WOULD HAVE been grateful! But the longer nothing happened, the more nervous I got about what might be *going to happen*. I thought about it last thing at night and first thing in the morning and in between, whenever my mind had nothing special to dwell on. (I got terrible marks that term, even for subjects I was usually good at like English and history.)

I couldn't tell Rosie or Tom I was frightened of *nothing*. I was too proud. I could have told the Pag, and I would have told her, if it hadn't been for what Rosie had said. If I told the Pag I was still scared of Willy, she might start thinking like Rosie. And the very last thing I needed was to give the Pag another reason why I should go to live with my mother and father!

I could write, *So I was alone with my fears!* But that would be making too much of a drama. And, anyway, it was much less horrific to make myself worry about what *might* happen with Willy than it was to think about what was *certainly* going to happen at half-term. Unless I got really seriously ill or died, or my parents died or were offered marvelous parts in an American film and had to take the next plane to Hollywood. . . .

In fact, by the time something did happen it was the last day before the half-term holiday, which made it seem less important than it later turned out to be. Because, of course, that was also the day before I was due to start my jail sentence on the other side of London, miles away from home comforts, from four dogs, and nine cats, and the Pag. . . .

I was late for school that morning. It was one of the Pag's London lecturing days, and she had already left when Mr. Wilberforce Frisbee turned up unexpectedly. Of all the Pag's patients he was the most obviously potty, dancing and singing in the street and waving his arms about as if he were conducting an orchestra, which had been his job before he went mad. On the other hand, he was usually friendly enough when you spoke to him, and except for little bursts of laughing at nothing, he could sometimes seem almost ordinary.

Not this morning, though. I found him on the porch when I opened the door, curled up among a lot of broken flower pots, looking like a bundle of old clothes someone had swept into the corner. When I bent over him, he made a moaning sound like the wind in the chimney.

I said, "She's not here, Mr. Frisbee. She wasn't expecting you. It isn't your day."

I got hold of his hand to help him up. I was afraid someone like the postman or the milkman would come and see him lying there and wonder why the Pag hadn't looked after him better. His hand was bony and hard and dreadfully cold. He gave a gasp and snatched it away from me, tucking it safe under his armpit, and tried to scrooge himself up even smaller.

I stood back so he could see I wasn't going to touch him again.

I said, "It's all right, Mr. Frisbee. It's only me, Catriona. You've seen me lots of times. I'm her granddaughter."

He quivered and shivered. I could hear his teeth chattering.

I said, "Come inside in the warm, Mr. Frisbee, and I'll make you a cup of tea."

He made that windy, wailing sound again and began scrabbling his feet on the tiles of the porch as if he might try to get up in a minute.

I said, "I'm going into the kitchen to put the kettle on."

I left the front door open, and the kitchen door. I lit the gas and filled the kettle. By the time it had begun to sing I could hear him in the hall. Not his usual light, dancing steps, but slow, timid, dragging ones. I put a mug for him on the table, the sugar bowl, the milk jug, the butter dish, and a loaf of bread. I cut four thick slices and put the sharp knife at the back of the kitchen drawer, "Just in case," I said to myself silently, as Mr. Wilberforce Frisbee came hesitantly into the kitchen, stopping just inside the door.

He didn't look dangerous. He looked old and dirty and sad. His hair was greasy and tangled and full of leaves and bits of twigs, and his clothes were filthy. I thought he should have a hot bath, but I didn't like to suggest it.

I said, "I ought to be going to school in a minute."

I made the tea and put the pot next to the mug and walked around the table very slowly so as not to startle him. He watched me carefully, his eyes glinting through his long, tangled hair, and when he saw what I was doing he shuffled around the table in the opposite direction and sat at the end of it.

I said, "That's right, Mr. Frisbee. You get some breakfast now. You don't have to be scared of me. I won't hurt you."

I went into the hall, only half closing the kitchen door in case he was afraid of being locked up like a prisoner, and ran out of the front door in time to stop Rosie coming in at the gate.

I said, "I'm going to be late for school, so you'll have to start off without me. Would you tell your mum that it's Mr. Frisbee, he's gone quite *doolally.* I mean, more than usual."

Rosie's mother didn't come at once. While I waited for her, I sat at the other end of the table in the kitchen and wished I could think of some way to help Mr. Frisbee. He was so terribly sad. He cried into his tea until his poor, wrinkled, dirty face was as wet as if he'd been caught in the rain. I told him a doctor was coming to help him, and that the Pag would be home by twelve o'clock at the latest unless she decided to go to the library after her lecture, but he only cried harder. In the end I got bored and hungry, just sitting there watching him, so I fried eggs for us both, two eggs each, and he had to stop crying in order to eat them. By the time Rosie's mother came, he was looking quite a lot less frightened and miserable.

Rosie's mother was breathless with hurrying. She had been out on a house call and had only just got the note Rosie had left her. I offered her a cup of tea but she said no, I must go to school and she would look after Mr. Frisbee until the Pag came back from London. She was seeing patients at eleven, but the practice nurse would help her keep an eye on him. He wouldn't be any trouble.

I hoped she was right, but I was more worried about how Mr. Frisbee might feel. He knew me, but he didn't know Rosie's mother or the practice nurse. Suppose he got frightened, alone with these strangers? But I was glad when he went off without making a fuss. I was sorry for Mr. Frisbee, but being alone with him had made me even more certain that just about the last thing I wanted to be when I grew up was a nurse or a doctor.

When I got to school it was midmorning break and everyone was out in the playground. I could hear the thundering and shrieking from halfway across the common and decided that teaching was another profession I meant to avoid. Imagine having to put up with that noise for almost the whole of your life! And the *smell*! Not just the cloakrooms, but certain individuals who carry their smell around with them. Like Fish Breath. There are always plenty of smelly Fish Breath people in schools. (In prisons, too, I should think, so being a prisoner or a prison warder doesn't figure in my future plans, either!)

I don't know what put Fish Breath into my head all of a sudden. The Pag says there is nothing supernatural about coincidence; it is all random chance. There may be only one chance in a thousand that you will think of a person and see him within the next couple of minutes, but when it does happen you will forget the nine hundred and ninety-nine chances, and only remember the one.

It gave me a shock, all the same. The instant I walked into the playground, there was Fish Breath, leaning against the wall with Willy beside him. They were laughing in a pleased, sneaky way that told me they had seen me before I saw them. I meant to pass with my nose in the air, but when Willy stuck out a foot to trip me up, I saw it in time to jump sideways.

This made them both laugh harder. Willy said, holding his ribs, "What's it like being a grass orphan?"

I didn't bother to answer. I had something more important to do at that moment. Because I hadn't come with a note from the Pag to my class teacher to say why I was late, I had to see Hairy Ears and explain. I expected to be in dead trouble; according to our headmaster, punctuality is a courtesy that underpins the whole structure of society. (He had actually written this in the leaflet we were sent before we came to the school. "Punctuality is the politeness of princes" is a neater way of putting it, the Pag said.)

To my surprise, he didn't lecture me today. Instead, he asked me a lot of questions about Mr. Frisbee and congratulated me on knowing how to look after him. He said, "Not many girls your age would know what to do with someone who is mentally ill."

I said, "You don't have to do all that much, really. Just listen, that's mostly what my grandmother does. Of course, you have to be sensible and hide things like guns."

Hairy Ears raised what would have been an eyebrow if he had eyebrows, creasing his pale, pudgy skin. He said, "*Guns*, Catriona?"

He knew I had made that up. It was a kind of boasting. I said quickly, "If you have them, I mean. All I did with Mr. Frisbee was put the bread knife at the back of the drawer. Just in case."

Hairy Ears nodded. He was doodling on the paper in front of him with a red ballpoint pen. Drawing circles. He said, "Were you frightened?"

"Not specially." It seemed a bit boring to say I hadn't been frightened at all. I said, "I would have been more frightened of some of the others."

He jerked his head up. "Is this something that happens often, Catriona? Your being left alone with one of these unfortunate people?"

He sounded as if he thought I was too young to behave like a sensible person, and that annoyed me. I might not have been absolutely on my own with one of the Pag's patients before, but I had opened the door to them, kept them company if the Pag was busy when they arrived, and though only old Flossie had come for

Christmas, the others had stayed for lunch or tea sometimes.

So I just shrugged my shoulders. "Not *very* often," I said. "My grandmother is usually there."

I was relieved that he hadn't given me a black mark for being so late. (When you had five black marks, your name was written in a book that was kept in the headmaster's office. None of the people in my class knew what happened after that; we just knew that a black mark was serious.)

Rosie said, "You should have got my mum to write a note for you. Then you wouldn't have had to go see him."

This was at lunchtime. We were lining up. I said, "I didn't mind. He was nice. What's a grass orphan?"

"He didn't call you that, did he?"

"'Course not. Willy did. Who d'you think?"

Rosie was silent a minute. Then she said, "I suppose, like a grass widow. A grass orphan isn't a real orphan, just a person whose parents are always away. Or not there."

"Silly Willy," I said. "Just the sort of silly thing he would think of."

Rosie frowned. "It's the sort of silly thing a grownup would think of. Not someone like Willy. It's not rude enough for that sort of boy. It's too sly—kind of sneering at you because you don't live with your mum and dad."

I laughed. "I don't want to live with them, do I? So Willy can sneer all he likes, it can't hurt me."

We were at the hatch by then. Lunch turned out to be a gourmet treat of baked beans and a big dollop of something brown with lumps in it that you would need to be a Nobel scientist to identify. The noise we all made as we sat at long tables to enjoy this delicate fare made it impossible to hear yourself speak, let alone have a real conversation. I thought, Rosie was right, *grass orphan* wasn't the kind of insult a boy like Willy would invent. Who had thought of it, then? Fish Breath? Or a much older person? Like Willy's horrible father?

I began to feel distinctly uncomfortable. *Grass orphan* wasn't as plain nasty as *Snotnose* or *Fish Breath*. Or even *Hairy Ears*, come to that. Although if I had been the sort of person who cared about being dumped by her mother and father, it might have upset me to be reminded.

I thought, *I must tell Rosie we are too old to be making up names for people. If she wants to go on with it, we must make a pact to only use them in private.*

I realized something for the first time. Rosie had started the naming of people, and it was she who had thought up the nastiest names. But she had only ever used them when she was talking to me. Unlike me, she had never called Willy "Snotnose" to his face. Unlike me, she never got into trouble. . . .

Even though I knew I was being unfair, I began to feel

hot and angry. I ate my lunch silently, eyes front. I didn't answer her when she spoke.

Rosie said, "Cat?"

She said, "What are we going to do after lunch?"

She said, "What's the matter?"

I answered then. I snarled, "Do you always have to be *perfect?*"

After that, we didn't speak to each other until school was over and we were tidying our desks and sorting out our books for half-term.

Rosie was finished before me. She had her coat on. She came and stood by my desk. She said, "I'm sorry, Cat."

She looked miserable and I felt ashamed. I tried to make a joke of it. "Don't be sorry," I said. "It's not your fault. You can't help being perfect."

I knew that was mean. But Rosie didn't complain, just hung her head. Which made her even more perfect, of course!

I gave up. I said, "It's me ought to say sorry. I don't want to go and stay with *them* and it's making me horrible."

"You're not horrible," Rosie said. "And I don't want you to go, either. Nor does Tom. Nor does my mum. She says it's not right to make you. I heard her say that to your grandmother yesterday evening. She came to borrow an onion."

I thought, *We've got loads of onions.* But it wasn't important. So I said, "What did the Pag say?"

"She didn't say anything, not that I heard. They stopped talking about you as soon as I came in the kitchen and your grandmother started on about onions. But I asked Mummy afterward and she said it was hard on your grandmother, your mother being her daughter. She can't fight for you as she'd like to."

I suppose I should have thought of that for myself. For a minute I thought, *The Pag should have told me!* But it didn't matter. I had been fairly sure that the Pag didn't want to get rid of me, but it was nice to hear it from someone sensible, like Rosie's mum!

I was in a really good mood as we went into the playground and waited for Tom by the gate. Rosie looked happy. Tom and I quite enjoyed fighting, but Rosie just hated it; she liked people to be pleasant together. I told myself I must try to remember that. I must try never to quarrel with Rosie.

Just as I came to this noble decision, I saw Willy and Fish Breath. They were hanging about on the other side of the gate, and they were looking at Rosie and me and whispering. Rosie and I never hurried at the end of the afternoon because it always took Tom a long time to get ready: to pack all the stuff he just *might* want sometime or other, tie his shoelaces, and get his coat on. He was usually the last of his class to appear, and today he was even later than usual. By the time he staggered out, there was hardly anyone left in the playground and only a few parents waiting outside in their cars.

Tom let go one of his bags to wave to us. As he tried to pick it up again, another bag fell. I said to Rosie, "I better give him a hand."

I dropped my own bag and started toward Tom. I had quite forgotten about Willy and Fish Breath, and when I ran past them and one of them stuck out a foot, I didn't see it in time. I got my balance before I hit the ground, but it made me feel stupid.

I whirled round and they were both grinning at me. "Grass orphan," Willy said, stretching his mouth wide with his thumbs and pulling the corners of his eyes down with his fingers. (This makes a horrible face: you don't have to take my word for it, you can try for yourself!) "Grass orphan," Willy said. "Grass orphan. Grass orph—*eeow!*"

He stopped with a yelp like a wild cat. Tom had shot past me, fast and hard as a bullet, and his head hit Willy smack in his middle. Then Willy was on the ground, on his back, and Tom was kneeling on top of him, clutching his head by his hair and thudding it on the concrete.

I expected Fish Breath to go for Tom, to help Willy. But Fish Breath was backing away, looking scared. And I was scared, too. I could hear the *crack* of Willy's head and the awful grunts he was making. I thought Tom would kill him.

I hurled myself forward. I pulled at Tom's jacket and shouted, "Stop it, Tom, stop it!" Tom paid no attention. I wailed, "Rosie. Help, Rosie . . ."

I don't know what happened then. Not exactly. I think Willy had managed to heave himself up a bit. Then I saw one of his hands under Tom's chin, bending Tom's head back, and the other hand jabbing up, hard fingers going straight for Tom's nose. No, not for Tom's nose. *For Tom's eyes.*

I got hold of Willy's hand somehow and wrenched it sideways and upward. His white wrist, with blue veins, was close to my face. I shut my eyes and bit it as hard as I could.

I heard him howl. And another voice shouting, a man's angry voice. Someone tugged my hair. Hard hands under my armpits jerked me back, lifted me off the ground, dumped me down. The man's voice said, "Oh, it's you again, is it?"

Willy was sniveling. Tom was standing beside him, red in the face, trying not to cry too. The man who had shouted was holding him by the collar.

He was a tall, thin man with a thin, foxy face. The very important school governor. Sir Archibald Wellington Plunkett Green. Willy's father.

Chapter Seven

"YOU HAVEN'T HEARD the last of this!"

Sir Archibald Wellington Plunkett Green fired this cheery parting shot over his shoulder as he marched Willy back into school to complain to Hairy Ears about our shocking behavior. I think he would have tried to take Tom and me along too if Rosie hadn't come to our rescue.

She had said, looking Willy's father in the eye and speaking firmly and clearly, "I saw everything that happened. It was Willy's fault, he started it. He tripped Catriona up and called her horrible names."

She had sounded so grown-up that Sir Archibald Wellington Plunkett Green probably thought she was much older than the rest of us. And since his son was

71

alive—and sniveling noisily, if not kicking—the Important School Governor could hardly arrest us for murder.

All the same, it was a relief when he took Willy's hand and left us alone. Even though he was still threatening us and purple with anger.

"He can't do anything," Rosie said. "I was the only witness. Fish Br—" She stopped herself. "I mean *the other one*, that friend of Willy's, he just ran off."

She looked at me. One of her secret looks; solemn, but with a hint of a smile, and I knew she had made up her mind to give up the name-calling at exactly the same time as me. Without either of us telling the other, or not aloud, anyway.

I wasn't surprised. It was the sort of thing that had been happening since we were about five and made poison together, mixing up dead worms and slimy leaves with pee in a jam jar. We kept the jar in Rosie's garden, hidden under a laurel bush. One day we talked about who we would poison and we both said "Tom," at exactly the same time, and giggled. Although I can't remember which of us kicked the jar over then, I know we each decided to get rid of the poison at the same moment, and without speaking.

It was one of the reasons we were best friends.

Another was that I could always rely on Rosie to talk our way out of trouble.

In the train going home, she said, "You'd better tell your gran what happened before you go off tomorrow. Then she can talk to Mummy over half-term and decide what to do if Mr. Baldry writes to complain."

It took me almost a minute to realize that Mr. Baldry was Hairy Ears.

I groaned—partly to stop myself laughing, partly because the torment that faced me this coming week made anything our bald-but-hairy-eared headmaster could do faded and feeble by comparison.

Tom said, "Nothing could be as bad as you think it is, Cat." And then, "Cheer up for Chatham, Dover's in sight," which was something his form teacher, Mr. Muckleberry, often said when he thought someone looked glum. No one knew what it meant, but Tom found it a useful thing to say when he couldn't think of anything better.

I said it to myself the next day, over and over, throughout the whole boring journey; the tube into London and the suburban train from Waterloo into Surrey. It was the same sort of thing as whistling in the dark to keep your courage up.

Both my mother and father were waiting for me at the station. As I crossed the footbridge, there was my mother, wobbling toward me on her high-heeled shoes, twittering like a bird. A cloud of disgusting scent billowed around me as she laid her powdery cheeks against my face, first one side then the other, kissing the air with a juicy sound. Then she held me away from her and said, "Oh my darlingest! What a wonderfully *brave* and *clever* angel child you are to come this long way on your own!"

I couldn't think how to answer that so I said nothing. But since I knew the Pag wanted me to try to be nice, I smiled weakly. My mother pinched my cheek—that is, she grabbed a lump of my flesh, hurting quite a bit, and shook it backward and forward—and said, "Daddy-O is *dying* to see his precious sweet honeybunch, so we must simply *fly*. He didn't dare leave the car in case some perfectly *beastly* person gave him a ticket."

Actually, Daddy-O was reclining comfortably in his seat with his eyes closed and his earphones on, beating time to the CD player. My mother opened the car door and shrieked at him, "She's *here*, you impossible man! Your own gorgeous baby daughter!"

My father opened his eyes and blinked at me. "Hi there," he said. He had a puzzled look, as if he wasn't totally sure who I was, and I knew he was still acting his part in *The Waiting Room*, the soap set in the retirement home that had at last brought my mother and father some fame and some fortune. My father played one of the younger inmates, a slightly forgetful but supposed-to-be-romantic widower who was a heartthrob for all the old ladies, and my mother was the matron, who had a soft spot for *him*.

My mother shook her head at him teasingly. She said, "Oh, you are a *slummocky* daddy!"

I said, "Hi there, Daddy-O."

I managed to say this without gagging. At least I didn't have to call my mother Mumsie! Although I had been born when she was over forty, she couldn't bear anyone to know she had a huge daughter my age. So when I had to call her something (which I avoided doing as much as possible), I called her by her name, which was Lisa.

Daddy-O winced and sighed as he sat upright and got out of the car. This was because the widower in the soap had arthritis and Daddy-O was almost too lazy to live; it was easier to pretend he had arthritis all the time than to change out of his part and be himself for a while.

"You get in the back, my own lambkin," my mother said, dabbing at my hair and tucking it behind my ears. "We're going to do a teensy-weensy bit of shopping, just a few things, then we'll take my sweetness to lunchy-munchy, a simply gorgeous little snuggery by the river, you'll love it, my angel!"

That's the way she talks most of the time. The only time she speaks like a human being is when she is having a row with Daddy-O. Or when she is buying cosmetics.

I won't write a blow-by-blow account of the rest of the morning because reading it would be as boring as living through it. All I will say is that most of the shopping was for stuff for my mother to put on her face, not in the daytime but at night—anti-wrinkle cream, that sort of thing. Nothing interesting about that, or not to me, except when I realized that she talked almost normally while she was choosing between one mind-bogglingly expensive jar and another. There were still a lot of *dearests* and *angels*, but the words in between were less silly.

She said as we left the last shop, tucking her hand under my elbow, "Sorry to be such a frightful bore, sweetheart, but an actor has to take care of her face, it's necessary upkeep, my darling."

The "simply gorgeous little snuggery" turned out to be an ordinary pub by the river. It was dark and smoky. "Lunchy-munchy" was gin for my mother, whisky for my father, and lots of packets of crisps and a cola for me. There was proper food at the bar, but by the time my father asked me if I would like something, both their faces had gone red and patchy from drinking and I thought it was time they were going.

My father sang in the car. He had a nice voice, but I think he sang to avoid bickering with my mother, who complained about his driving. She said he was "wandering all over the road." She screeched when he went through a red light, and he shouted back at her. I tightened my seatbelt and braced my feet on the floor. My father was watching me in the driving mirror. He said,

"Daddy-O's a good driver, he'll get you home safe, don't you pay any heed to her, poppet."

"Home" was a smart new house that had a paved front garden without grass or flowers. (No old dustbins or broken flowerpots, either.) Inside it was so clean I wondered if I should take my shoes off, and the sofa and the armchairs were covered with slippery pink satin that looked as if no one had ever sat on it. (No dogs, of course, no cats, not even a goldfish or a canary.)

No rings on the furniture. No ashtrays. No bookshelves. No books. Lots of photographs of my mother and father on the mantelpiece, on every table, hanging on every wall.

The carpets were palest gray; as I followed my mother upstairs I glanced back to see if my feet had left marks. The room where I was to sleep was all yellow—plain yellow walls and a yellow carpet, yellow flowers on the curtains and the bed cover. I put my duffle bag on the bed, where it looked old and grubby.

"You've got your own bathroom, my angel," my mother said, opening a yellow door. "Won't that be *fun?*"

She didn't wait for me to speak, which was lucky. (What could I have said? How could a bathroom be *fun?*) She was busy pulling out drawers, showing me how the closets opened. (Just like any old closets is the answer to that.) She said, "*There* you are, dearest one. Make yourself cozy. Daddy-O and I are going to have a little nappikins because we're having a little party this evening. All the cast is coming, all our friends, just to meet our dear little daughter."

And she went out and closed the door behind her.

I heard her open another door and close it. I heard my father come up the stairs and open the same door (at least, it made the same sound) and close it again. After that, nothing. Nothing at all.

I unpacked the duffle and put my clothes away and tried to read, but I wasn't comfortable in my yellow room. It was like being shut up inside a daffodil. I opened the door and crept out, but when I got downstairs I didn't dare sit anywhere or touch anything. I would have liked to ring the Pag to say I had arrived safely, but by the time I had found the telephone, hidden under a doll with silk skirts, the quiet in the house had really unnerved me. I was afraid of clearing my throat, let alone talking. I found the telly inside a polished cabinet with more glamorous portraits of my parents standing on top of it, but I couldn't turn it on in case it woke them up. I wanted a drink of water and I found a glass in the clean, scrubbed, silent kitchen, but I was afraid it would make a terrible noise if I turned on the tap. In the Pag's house—*at home*—when you ran a bath or flushed the lavatory, the water thundered and crashed in the pipes as if there had been some enormous natural disaster, a tidal wave or a quake that might open the earth and swallow us up. The Pag was always saying she must have it seen to but she never did. She said there always seemed to be something more amusing to do than play about with the plumbing.

I went back to my yellow room.

I sat on the bed.

And waited.

I read a chapter of *Jane Eyre*.

And waited.

Then I changed into my black velvet miniskirt and white cashmere sweater.

And waited some more.

The house was dead quiet for *five hours*.

At the end of the longest afternoon of my life, there was *pandemonium*. Of course, they had slept too long! I should have woken them up! The party was due to start in just under an hour! They would never be ready in time!

They flew around the house, banging doors, swearing and yelling—at each other, at me. I couldn't see what the fuss was about. Reconnoitering in the kitchen during their interminable siesta, I had noted the bottles of wine in the fridge and the plates of party nibbles covered with transparent plastic. But my mother was gasping and sobbing and putting the back of her hand to her forehead as if she was auditioning for a part in some exceptionally harrowing tragedy.

"I can't do it," she moaned. "I simply can't do it! I'm not even dressed!"

Daddy-O had disappeared at this point so I was her only audience. I tried to think what the Pag would like me to do.

I said, "I can put the food out. I can pour drinks. I can answer the door. There's nothing else to do, is there?"

She stopped her act instantly. "Oh," she said. "*Oh duckie,* will you really? What a perfect *angel pie* you are!"

She tripped merrily out of the kitchen and vanished upstairs.

Daddy-O appeared a few minutes later. He was wearing tight purple trousers and a white shirt with big, billowing sleeves. This fancy gear made him look older. I thought— I couldn't be sure—that he was wearing lipstick.

He saw me looking at him. He said, "Your mother likes to dress up." He wasn't apologizing. Just explaining.

I said, "That's a beautiful shirt, Daddy-O."

I thought, *The Pag would be proud of me!* I had meant to behave badly, but it was turning out to be harder than I had expected. It would have been like being beastly to a couple of little kids.

She came down the stairs then, pausing at the bottom to twirl around so that the skirt of her red dress flew out, showing her black lace tights right up to her bottom.

Daddy-O caught her round the waist and danced her round the hall. I stood at the kitchen door and watched them. Her hair had been sprayed so hard it didn't move, and the false hair that covered his bald patch was stiff and woolly.

Suddenly I knew what they reminded me of. A pair of Barbie dolls!

A giggle burst out of me, I couldn't help it, but as the door chimes sang at that moment I was able to turn it into a wildly excited laugh as I ran to the door.

The party might have been worse. I carried plates of food around and helped Daddy-O refill people's glasses. I can't say the evening exactly passed in a flash, but it was less boring than I had expected.

Although I had never met any of the guests before, they were not exactly strangers because I had seen most of them on television. In a way, each one of them seemed like two people to me: the character in the soap and the person who was taking peanuts out of the bowl I was holding. At least, that was how it was to begin with. But once I talked to them, it was different. The actress who played the oldest inhabitant of the retirement home stopped being an old lady who kept falling asleep and losing her glasses and turned into a much younger person who didn't need spectacles and said she had a daughter not much older than me.

A couple of them seemed to be the same people in life as they were on the screen. I wasn't sure if they had been given their parts because that was the sort of people they were or if, like Daddy-O with his arthritis, they had decided it was easier to stay as their television characters than go in for the bother of changing back to their real selves.

Or perhaps they got muddled about who they were *really*.

There was an almost-young man—that is, not as old as the others—who played one of the doctors who regularly visited the retirement home. He was supposed to be in love with my mother. I mean, he was in love with *the matron*. I mean, he was in love with her *in the serial*. I poured more wine into his glass later on in the evening (although he had already had enough, in my opinion!) and he said, in the same shy way he had when he was acting the doctor, "I hope you know you have a wonderful mother!"

And I knew he was in love with her in real life. Now. At this party.

I said, because I had to say something, "She is very pretty. And a very good actress."

But it made me feel strange. And lonely for the Pag.

I got even lonelier as the week went by. I telephoned

the Pag once every day and I thought she sounded lonely too, though of course she didn't say so. I would have telephoned her more often, but I guessed she would worry if I did that, in case it should upset my parents. Though *parents* was an odd word to describe Lisa and Daddy-O. It seemed to me that *children* would be better!

That week, I felt as if they got younger and younger as I got older and older. They quarreled like babies. He pulled her hair when she annoyed him! She pinched him and then ran away, squealing. They snatched the newspaper from each other in the way little kids sometimes snatch each other's toys.

They were nice to me; that is, they were nice to me when they remembered I was there. They were rehearsing most days, either in the morning, which meant they left the house before I was awake, or in the afternoon, in which case they didn't come out of their bedroom until about eleven. For about the first twenty-four hours I wasn't sure what they expected me to do. After that, I knew they didn't expect anything in particular.

When they came home in the evening, my mother put her feet up on the sofa and had what she called a "drinkie-pinkie," and Daddy-O cooked the supper. Sometimes I helped Daddy-O and sometimes I sat with my mother while she drank her gin. I asked them what they had been doing all day but they never asked me. They were not interested in what happened to me when they were not there.

Ringing up Rosie was one of the things I did when I was left on my own. I said, "It's as if *I'm* not there when they aren't! As if I only existed when they could see me."

"Are you hungry?" Rosie wanted to know. "I could bring you some food. I expect Mummy would let me come if I said they were starving you."

She sounded hopeful, as if she were as bored as I was this holiday. And I would have loved her to come. But even if she only came for the day (carrying her basket of goodies like Little Red Riding Hood), Lisa and Daddy-O might come home early and catch her. And although I thought they were a comical pair, I didn't want Rosie to laugh at them.

I said, "There's masses of food in the freezer. And the person who comes to clean cooks lunch for me. Don't tell the Pag what I said about not existing. I'm fine, really."

The person who came to clean was called Fitz. Short for Fitzroy. He was an actor who was out of work at the moment.

"Resting, dear, that's what we say in the theater. So I make a crust, cleaning."

He was very cheerful, thin, and quite young. He had a dreadful cough. He cooked spaghetti for me on my last day and sat with me and chain-smoked while I ate it, leaving the kitchen door open to take the smell away. I knew it was none of my business. But I said, all the same, "You ought to eat something, Fitz. It might stop you smoking so much."

He made a face, rolling his eyes up. "Heaven protect me from crusading young females. I get enough of that from my mother."

I was embarrassed. I felt myself going red and that embarrassed me more. I said, "Sorry. It's a terrible habit I've got. It's just, my grandmother smokes, and I keep trying to stop her."

No use apologizing. Fitz was much too offended. He pushed back his chair and stood up, indignantly shaking his long, shiny ponytail. He said, "Well, you'll be spared the trouble, Miss Bossy Boots, when you come to live here."

He swept his cigarettes off the table and buttoned the packet into his shirt pocket. "Smoking is a worse crime than murder in your mother's and father's opinion. No sin in *gin*, on the other hand, and your father drinks whisky like a baby drinks milk. If they're entitled to their vice, I'm entitled to mine, that's how I look at it."

"I don't care how you look at *anything*," I said rudely. (He had been rude, after all.) But I didn't want to waste time arguing about smoking and drinking. There was something more important I had to get straight.

"I'm not coming to live here. Where'd you get that idea?"

He looked astonished. "They told me, of course. 'Won't it be lovely, Fitz? Our own little girl! Her grandmother's not too happy about it, but she hasn't a leg to stand on.'"

If I hadn't been watching him, I would have thought it was my mother speaking. Only he made her sound even sillier. I thought, *He must hate her.*

I said, "What do you mean? I *live* with my grandmother. It's where I live. It's my *home.* They can't make me leave it. I don't *want* to be here."

I was frantic suddenly. Fitz was only saying these things to get back at me. If I hadn't been rude to him, this wouldn't be happening. I said, "I didn't mean to be nasty."

But it was no good. Even though he had stopped being angry, it didn't make any difference. He said, speaking quite gently, "I thought they'd have told you. They've made their minds up. Or your mother has, and your father does what she says. They've been to see a lawyer to fix it up. Your mother told me. 'She may be a teeny bit upset to begin with, but she's old enough now not to need too much looking after.'"

Then he grinned and said in his own voice, "You're old enough to be useful, too. Fetch the gin, wash the dishes. Only she wouldn't say that to me, naturally."

"I won't come," I said. I got up from the table. "I'm

going to pack and I'm going home now. I'm not coming back ever again. They can't make me."

He looked at me sadly. "You poor little cocker. They're your mum and dad. They can do what they like with you."

Chapter Eight

I DIDN'T RUN AWAY for two reasons. I had no money to run away *on*. And I hadn't finished the book I was reading.

I had spent all my pocket money as well as the emergency money the Pag had given me on books and sweets to comfort myself in my lonely exile. I did find some books in the house in the end—stashed away in a cardboard box in a poky little attic at the top of a flight of narrow stairs. I didn't find this stairway for several days because it was hidden by a door that looked like an ordinary closet door. Although I had been snooping around fairly intensively, I had no particular interest in the towels or sheets I had assumed my parents kept there.

There wasn't anything very interesting in the contents

of the attic when I finally got there. No old photographs, no birth certificates, no yellowing letters, no significant wills—in fact, disappointingly, not a single document that might prove I was a foundling or, better still, an orphan of royal birth. Just some smart-looking suitcases, a sofa that had nothing obviously wrong with it, a chest of summer clothes all very neatly packed between sheets of tissue paper, and this box of books. They were mostly books about the theater, biographies of actors and actresses, but there also were a couple of Agatha Christies I hadn't read. As I had finished the paperbacks I had bought and had run out of money, they just about saved my reason.

Since I had no money, I was going to have to try to hitchhike, which might mean a lot of hanging about at the sorts of places lorry drivers might stop at for a cup of tea. (I knew I shouldn't accept lifts from strangers, but this was an emergency, and I thought lorry drivers were probably safer than people in cars.) Waiting until the right sort of truck driver showed up would be boring without a book. To begin with, I thought I could just take the Agatha Christie with me and post it from home. But then, I thought, I would have to write a note to say I had taken it. The Pag was very stern about borrowing other people's books without permission.

And I didn't want to have anything to do with my mother and father *ever again*.

So I settled down to the last few chapters and they took longer than I'd expected. As I finished the last page, I heard the front door and my mother's voice. "Cooee, sweetie pie." I froze, and she called again. "Special din-dins tonight, pussy willow, come and give us a handy-pand?"

(Writing this down, I am incredulous. How can any human being talk like that? There ought to be a law against it.)

Although my heart gave a thump—as if she had caught me out doing something I shouldn't—I was relieved, really. While I had been finishing the Agatha Christie, the largest part of my mind had been working out the *for*s and *against*s of running away this evening instead of leaving tomorrow and finding more and more *against*s, the chief *against* being that the Pag would say it was rude and unkind to run away without saying goodbye and thank you for having me.

All the same, my heart gave a few more thumps as I went downstairs. I needed to know if what Fitz had told me was true: Did they really—honestly, truly—want me to stay with them forever? Was it true they could *make* me? How could they make me? But I knew I would be too afraid to ask them these questions straight out.

Would it be best to smile and be nice so *they* would be nice to *me* and let me go home to the Pag forever and ever? Or should I behave so horribly that they would never want to see me again?

I didn't do either. I ate the "special din-dins" even though it was takeaway Chinese which I found fairly disgusting, but I didn't talk much, and I think I must have looked sad or grumpy because my mother said suddenly, "You know, Daddy-O, I think Precious-Kins wants to stay with us!"

I didn't say anything, just looked at my plate, numb and dumb with horror.

Daddy-O said, "Oh, for Heaven's sake, leave the kid alone, Lisa."

And followed up this unnaturally normal remark by getting up from the table and saying to me, "Come on, Catty, let's get these things in the dishwasher."

That was almost the end of the evening. I kept looking at the clock and wondering how early I could pretend to be sleepy. When the news came on at nine o'clock, Daddy-O switched off the television and stood up, yawning and stretching. He said, "Morning call tomorrow, so we'll get you to the station early, kiddo."

And my mother said, "Off to bed with you, chicken."

I was surprised. I had been afraid they would make much more fuss on my last evening. I was so relieved that I let them both kiss me good night without turning my head away and said politely, "Thank you so much for having me."

They both smiled then—but at each other, not at me—and when I got to my room I understood why.

There was a pile of presents on my yellow bed, each one wrapped in gold paper and tied with gold and scarlet ribbon.

There was a pink and blue travel bag with soap and shampoo and toothpaste and a hairbrush and comb. There was a neat travel clock with a flap that opened to show you the time in different parts of the world. There was a camera in a leather case. There was a blue and green top and trousers made of lovely, slippery, silky material and a pair of matching slippers with gold buckles. There was an envelope with two ten-pound notes in it and a book token for thirty pounds.

I could bear it all until I got to the book token. All the other presents were the sort of things you might give to anyone. That is, people like my parents might give to anyone. The book token meant they—or one of them, anyway—had actually *noticed* at least one thing about me.

It made me want to cry. Until then, I had been angry. I had almost made up my mind that I was going to leave these presents behind. (Most of them anyway. Not the camera, perhaps. And I had thought I might try the blue and green trousers and top. Just to see if they fitted.)

Now I saw that I couldn't just shove all these things away in the closet and pretend I had never seen them. I had to pack them all in my duffle bag and take them home—and before I went home, I would have to say thank you.

I thought, *It's not fair.* I felt it wasn't fair, somehow, though I couldn't altogether see why. And this made me angry again.

✧

I was still angry when I woke up in the morning. I was angry when I said thank you for all the presents. I don't think they noticed; they were too busy getting ready for their rehearsal. I was even angrier by the time I got on the train, and it got worse and worse, so that by the time I met the Pag at our station I was boiling.

I didn't smile at her. I didn't say hello. She had brought Wilkins-the-Mongrel to meet me, and I pushed him away when he jumped up at me. I marched straight past them both, up the stairs, into the station yard. The old car was waiting at the curb. I wrenched open the back door and hurled my duffle bag in. I slammed the door. I flung myself round to face the Pag and said, "Don't you ever lock the car? Someone will steal it one day and then you'll be sorry."

I thought, *If she laughs, I will kill her!* But she didn't laugh. She put her hand on my shoulder and said, "I'm sorry, Cat, I've got bad news for you. Old Boot is dead."

So it was all right to cry. The Pag put Wilkins-the-Mongrel into the back and we got in the front, and although she wasn't much of a cuddler in the ordinary way she cuddled me now, holding me tightly and telling me what exactly had happened. She had found the old pug dead in his basket that morning, looking as peaceful as if he were sleeping. "He didn't suffer," the Pag said. "He was old, and he died of old age, very gently and easily."

I said, "I know, I *know*, we should all be so lucky." The Pag did laugh then. I had been crying so hard, tears and snot were bubbling out of my nose, and she wiped my face with her handkerchief as though I were a baby.

She said, "All right now?" and I nodded. I was glad she didn't ask why I had been so angry when she first saw me, because I wouldn't have known how to answer her. Wilkins, who had been whining softly behind us, stood with his paws on the back of the seat and licked the backs of our necks, tickling and making us shiver.

I wasn't angry anymore. I said, "I missed you. I'm glad I'm back."

She said, "I missed you, too," and started the car.

That was Saturday. It wasn't until the next day that we had a proper conversation. She didn't ask what had happened, and I didn't say. But around seven o'clock Sunday evening, she put her head around the door to say supper was ready, and I showed her the presents my parents had given me.

She said, "That's a very fine camera."

She said, "The blue and green suits you. Lovely for parties."

She said, "Useful wash bag. And that's a good travel clock. Now you're equipped to cross the Sahara!"

She said, "All right, all right—you'll need a camel as well."

I showed her the book token. She said, "You must admit, they are making an effort."

I said, "I don't want to go there again. I won't go. I don't have to, do I?"

The Pag sighed. She said, "Cat . . ."

I said, "Please. *Please!* PLEASE!"

The Pag sat on my bed. She was wearing one of her black skirts and a pair of heavy lace-ups that made her ankles look extra delicate and thin. She was thinner all over; her cheek bones jutted out and her nose had got beakier.

I said, "You haven't been eating properly!"

I picked up her wrist and pinched up the loose skin. I said, "I go away for a week and just look at you."

She said, "That'll do, Cat. I look after you, that's the way it is, not the other way round."

I said, "Is it true they can make me go there and live with them? You don't want me to, do you? It's not a *law*, is it?"

The Pag took my hands and held them. She said, "Forget about the law. And leave me out of it. Think about yourself. You could be happy with them once you got used to it."

I pulled my hands away and put them over my ears, pressing the flaps in as hard as I could. I said, "I asked you about the law. I said, 'Is it the law?' You answer me about that and I'll listen."

She sighed, very deeply. She said, "Let's have supper first. I've made lasagna and it'll spoil if we leave it."

The Pag was a good cook when she wanted to be. I said, when I had mopped my plate clean after a huge second helping, "Makes a nice change from made-up frozen meals and takeaways."

She said, "No point in cooking unless you enjoy it. Nothing wrong with frozen food. You and I have takeaways sometimes. And dog rusks for breakfast. So you told your teacher, apparently."

I couldn't think what she meant. Then I remembered. I said, "But I love them, you know that. They're yummy. Nicer than fresh bread."

"I know that," the Pag said. "Others don't. Your teacher among them."

I was puzzled. We didn't have half-term reports. And no one had given me a letter to take home to the Pag.

She said, "I had a visitor while you were away. Mr. Baldry. Your headmaster."

I said, without thinking, "Hairy Ears!"

"True," the Pag said. "Though not the politest of observations. And, indeed, Mr. Baldry seemed to think you were not as polite as you might be to some of the other people at school."

"That's not fair! It's not me, or not *just* me. Rosie started it! I just couldn't tell *him* that, not when he told me off, could I? I mean, tell on Rosie. And we've stopped anyway! We stopped at the end of last term."

The Pag nodded. "I told him there was usually a natural end to that kind of behavior."

She looked at me, wondering if I had understood her. "That is, things wear themselves out. He seemed to think you had it in for one particular boy. Persecuting him, picking fights, as well as name-calling. I reminded him that it wasn't one-sided. That I'd had occasion to tell this boy off because he and his friends had been bullying you. And your headmaster said he knew about what he called 'that unfortunate incident.' He said William Green's father had complained that I'd frightened the boy. I said I was sorry."

"You *what?*"

"You were scared of him and it made me so angry that I forgot he was only a child, not a monster."

"He's a monster child," I said, and she laughed.

"Perhaps. But I am supposed to be a grownup. And a very *old* grownup."

I said, "You're not old."

"Oh, but I am. And old people get careless."

She was smiling but she was upset, I could see. She said, "The real reason your headmaster came to see me was to say he was worried about you. Someone had told him that I see some of my patients at home, now I am retired from the hospital, and that you are alone with them sometimes. He had come to tell me he thought you were too young to be left on your own with mad people. I couldn't think what he was talking about to begin with. Then I remembered the day Mr. Frisbee made you late for school. But you weren't alone for long, were you? And it was only Mr. Frisbee. . . ."

She was thinking aloud, frowning and anxious. I remembered what I had said to Mr. Baldry about hiding knives and guns. I said, "It's such a fuss if you're late at that school. You've got to have a good excuse."

I waited for her to speak but she didn't. I said, feeling indignant suddenly, "I only told him I put the knife at the back of the drawer! So he wouldn't hurt himself. That's what I meant."

Was it what I had said, though? I couldn't remember.

She looked at me. She was half smiling, but her eyes were sad.

She said, "At least we've been forewarned."

"What d'you mean?"

(It seems stupid now, looking back, but I really didn't understand.)

She said, in a gentle voice, "If they want to take you away, they have a good case. We could argue about my being too old to look after you. But it's not only that I give you dog food for breakfast. The life I apparently lead, surrounded by dangerous lunatics, is not one that a young girl should be expected to share."

I wailed, "But it's not *like* that. You know it isn't. They can't take me away and make me live in their horrible house—as if I was a piece of *furniture* or something!"

I remembered what Fitz had told me. They were my mother and father. They could do what they liked with me. I said, "I know they've been to see a lawyer. Can't we have one too, and stop it all happening?"

"We could," the Pag said. "But we are not going to." She stood up and started collecting the dishes. She came behind me and put her hand on my shoulder. She said, "I love you. I love my daughter. I would like you to love each other. This way there is at least a chance that we might all continue to speak to one another."

She had said "my daughter." Until now, she had always called her "your mother" or Lisa. And it made something horribly clear to me.

The Pag might say she loved me. But she must love *her* more.

I wanted to shout and swear and stamp and scream. But I said nothing. I sat still and stared at my dirty plate.

The Pag stroked the back of my neck. She said, "I

promise you, Cat, I'll do all I can. You'll come and stay. We'll go to Greece, just as always. You'll just have two homes, not one. And three people to take care of you."

"Oh, brilliant!"

I tried to snarl but it turned into a croak. I twisted round in my chair and buried my face in the Pag's stomach and she held my head tight for a long time, without speaking.

Chapter Nine

I MADE ALL SORTS OF PLANS. I would run away to Greece. I had enough money in my post office savings bank for a cheap air ticket. Or I could get the train through France and Italy and catch the ferry from Ancona to Patras and then the local bus. I had my own passport, and Eleni and Kostas, who kept the taverna, had the key to the house.

The trouble with that plan was that the whole village knew me. One telephone call and Interpol would be hot on my heels. I would be flown back to England—in handcuffs most probably—and there would be pictures of me on the television news. The Pag would be mortified.

It would be safer, as well as easier, to disappear into London and sleep in shop doorways or inside cardboard boxes like all the other runaway children. I had a warm sleeping bag so I wouldn't freeze to death.

But Rosie was sure they would track me down very quickly. "Most of those kids, their families don't care," she said. "Your grandmother's different. She'd keep on at the police till they found you."

Another way to hide would be to go to a different part of the country, Manchester or Glasgow, and get a job cooking or cleaning in someone's house or looking after their children. There were always lots of advertisements for nannies and household helps in the newspapers.

But Rosie said, "You don't look old enough. No one would employ you except the sort of people who beat their servants and starve them and keep them locked up when they're not working. And your grandmother would put your picture just about everywhere, outside police stations and on the telly."

She had a better idea, naturally. There was a space under the roof in her house where we had sometimes played when we were younger, making a camp under the eaves and hiding from Tom. But no one used the roof space now and it was too cramped and awkward for storage.

"So it's just right to hide in," Rosie said. "There's enough room to put a sleeping bag on the other side of the water tank, and I'd bring you food secretly."

I pointed out that there were other physical necessities besides eating and sleeping. If Rosie was too nice-minded to mention that I might need to go to the lavatory, I wasn't so niminy-piminy! She said, a bit crossly, that of course she had thought of it. I could creep down to the bathroom when the house was empty, or in the middle of the night, and have a pot for emergencies.

I snorted. Rosie sighed. She said, "There is *one* thing you could do. I did ask my mum, so it's probably true. But it does seem . . ."

She looked unsure of herself. Unlike Rosie.

"Does seem what?"

"Oh, I don't know. Just, I don't think *I* could . . ."

I said, "If you go on like that I'll go *ape*."

And I scratched under my armpit and gibbered.

Rosie said sternly, "You shouldn't mock animals."

"Monkeys aren't animals. They're our close cousins."

"We're animals, moron," Rosie said.

"Okay, *okay*," I said. "If you're so frightfully, wonderfully clever, perhaps you wouldn't mind using your brilliant brain cells to tell me what this *one thing* was that your mum said I could do! Using words of one syllable so that this feeble-minded person might have a distant, faraway, *outside* chance of knowing what you were talking about! And, since you're so sensitive about apes, you might remember that dummies like me have some feelings, too!"

Rosie grinned. "All right, pea brain. My mum said you

could go to a solicitor. Any solicitor, like in the High Street. Mum says it's a new law that they have to listen to children about where they want to live and who they want to live with, that sort of thing. Mum says they made this new law because of people getting divorced more often than they used to."

I said, "My parents aren't getting divorced."

Rosie rolled her eyes up in despair at my utter stupidity. "It's grandparents, too. Aunts and uncles. You just have to say who you want to stay with. There has to be a reason, like with you and your grandmother. I mean, she's looked after you almost all of your life. But my mum says it's hard for her to go to law against her own daughter."

I thought of going to law. Of a judge in a scarlet robe and a wig sitting high above the court and peering over half-moon spectacles at the people below. I said, "I could go in the witness box and swear on the Bible that I wanted to live with the Pag."

All at once, I was hugely excited. I said, "Would they really let me do that? Would they *listen*?"

"I don't know," Rosie said. She was looking uncomfortable suddenly. "Mummy only said—well, she said that a person in your situation could ask a solicitor. I don't think she was serious. I don't mean she was making it up, but you know what she's like. She was just telling *me* so I'd know. Going on in the way she does when we ask things. I mean, I don't think she meant me to tell you."

She was sorry she had, I could see. Rosie didn't like trouble. And she was afraid that trouble was just what she'd started.

I said, "It's okay! You don't have to help. I won't say where I got the idea, I won't give you away. So you can just forget that you told me."

I suppose I was angry. I should have known Rosie better. She might not like trouble, but she would never leave me to face it alone.

She said, with a martyred sigh, "Of course I'll come with you. I look older than you do, and if I'm not there you might say something silly."

Once you start looking, there are solicitors everywhere. I had never noticed before that there was a solicitor's office outside the tube station, and two in the High Street, and one over the hardware store down the alley next to the little supermarket that was open every day until midnight. All the other offices had big, clean windows and smart entrances, but the one in the alley had only a shabby door at the side of the hardware store, with a dirty brass letter box and a card above the bell that said, in block letters, PERKINS AND TWINKLE.

"No," Rosie said. "They don't look respectable. Not . . ." She frowned, looking for the right word. "Not powerful enough," she said finally. "I mean, you're only a child, so you need someone who looks extra strong and important."

The firm she fixed on had an office in the High Street, next to Woolworth's. It was called Malcolm, Page and Threadneedle. Rosie said, "The Bank of England is in Threadneedle Street." I didn't see what this had to do with anything, but I kept quiet because I thought Rosie might know something I didn't and I was bored with her making me feel I was ignorant.

We decided to visit Malcolm, Page and Threadneedle on Wednesday afternoon, on our way home from school. I wanted Tom to come too, but Rosie said three of us might make it look like some kind of game, or a dare. So we told Tom we were going to McDonald's and we had something private to talk about. He didn't seem to mind. It was his birthday in March, and perhaps he thought we wanted to discuss his presents. (Or maybe he didn't think about it at all. How should I know? Just because you are writing a book doesn't mean you have to know everything.) All I can be sure of is that he didn't make a fuss, just grinned and went on home, whistling.

Malcolm, Page and Threadneedle was the grandest of all the solicitors. The name was engraved in gold on the window, and the receptionist sat high up inside a glass cage that I decided must be bulletproof because it looked so thick. I stood on tiptoe and said, "I'd like to speak to Mr. Threadneedle, please." Rosie prodded me and I added quickly, "Or Mr. Malcolm or Mr. Page, if Mr. Threadneedle is busy."

The receptionist had a soft, wobbly bosom, big dark glasses, and an enormous blond Afro that stuck out so far on either side of her face that it almost touched the sides of her glass cage. She looked startled—as if she hadn't expected me to speak English—and I could feel Rosie shaking beside me as she began silently giggling.

The receptionist shook her head and her hair quivered. She put up a hand and patted it. Her fingernails were about two inches long and painted green to match her eyelids. She said, "None of the partners see clients without an appointment. But I hardly think you can be a client, little girl."

She had a hoity-toity voice. She was so pleased with herself. She thought that calling me "little girl" would make it quite clear to me that I was no one of any importance. Perhaps she expected me to curl up and die of shame at being called female and young!

I said, "I'm not a client yet. But if I may see one of the solicitors, I might be a client quite soon."

Rosie said boldly, "We don't mind waiting until someone is free. This is an emergency."

The receptionist looked at her and frowned in a puzzled way. Then she said, "I know who you are, young woman. Your mother's my doctor. Does she know what you're up to?"

"It's me who wants a solicitor," I said.

But she ignored me. She leaned forward so that her bosom squashed on the edge of the desk and spoke to Rosie in a voice that was slithery and slimy with spite. "Run along now, dear, and take your naughty little friend with you. Unless you want me to ring up your mummy and tell her you've been making a nuisance of yourself in the High Street!"

Rosie said we shouldn't have gone in our school uniform, but I thought it wouldn't have made any difference to the way we'd been treated at Malcolm, Page and Threadneedle.

I said, "They're too posh for us. You'd have to be covered in furs and diamonds to get past that horrible *creature*. I don't think she's *human*. Human beings don't have green fingernails. She's an alien."

Rosie said. "My mum said it was the law that they had to listen to children. So she was breaking the law."

We had turned down the alley. Outside Perkins and Twinkle, Rosie said, "Would it be better if you went on your own? I could wait in McDonald's."

"Coward," I said. "You started this. You stick with me."

The bell didn't work. I pushed at the door and it opened. There was an old, flyspecked notice on the wall with a hand pointing up.

108

COME STRAIGHT UP IF BELL OUT OF ORDER.
WAITING ROOM ON THE LEFT. LAVATORIES ON THE RIGHT.

The stairs were narrow and dusty and dark. At the top, the door to the waiting room stood open. There was a table with magazines on it, and an old man asleep in a chair in one corner with his mouth open. There were two other doors. One was the lavatory. The other had a lion's head for a knocker.

"Go on," Rosie said.

I banged and the door shook. There was a click and a whir and it opened. More dusty stairs and a woman's voice coming down. "If that's you, Mr. Hornswaddle, don't worry, I'll be down in a minute."

"It's me," I said. My mouth was dry. "Catriona Brooke. I need to talk to a solicitor. It's about something important. Are you Miss Twinkle?"

"Miss Perkins. My partner is Mr. Twinkle." The owner of the voice stood at the top of the stairs. She was a short, stout person, old but not *very* old (older than Rosie's mum but younger than the Pag), and she had a lot of pale hair that looked, with the light shining behind her, as if she were wearing a halo.

She said, "Please come up to my office, Miss Brooke. And bring your friend with you."

She spoke as if it was the most natural thing in the world that two first-form girls in school uniform should want to see a solicitor.

There were two doors at the top of the stairs, but only one room: a long room, high as a barn, with light streaming in through big skylights, walls covered with books, and floor covered with piles of paper. A tall, thin man (about three times the height and half the width of Miss Perkins) was standing on a stepladder, reaching up to the top shelf of a bookcase.

He said, "Come in, come in, mind where you put your feet, we're busy reorganizing, at least that's what Miss Perkins calls it, making a mess out of what was a highly efficient and tidy muddle, that's what *I* say."

He brushed his hands together to get rid of the dust and came down the stepladder. He looked carefully at Rosie and me, head on one side, for a minute, then said, "Do you think there can be such a thing as a tidy muddle? I daresay you'd call it a contradiction in terms. Still, I don't suppose you've come for a philosophical discussion, so let's get down to the nitty-gritty. Sit you down, both of you, find a chair, chuck the stuff off it, take a pew."

He said all this perfectly seriously, but I think he meant to make us laugh because when we did he nodded in a pleased way. He sat behind a desk and put his elbows on it, looked at us with a broad and delighted smile, and said, "How can we help you?"

I didn't know how to answer. It seemed unlikely that they could help me at all. These funny people! This untidy room!

Miss Perkins said, "Mr. Twinkle is quite sensible, really, Miss Brooke."

Her eyes were shiny and bright, and I knew *she* knew what I was thinking and it made me ashamed. Although I couldn't help my thoughts, I should have hidden them better. I was so upset to think I might have hurt Miss Perkins and Mr. Twinkle that it was suddenly quite easy to tell them about the Pag and my mother and father.

Telling them made me cry. I couldn't stop. I said, "I'm sorry."

Rosie took my hand. Miss Perkins passed me a packet of tissues and said, "I think I had better go down and see Mr. Hornswaddle. Did you see him in the waiting room, girls? Was he asleep?"

I was grateful to her for ignoring my sniffles and snuffles. I said, "Fast asleep. He didn't wake when we knocked the knocker."

Mr. Twinkle was scribbling away in a big notebook that was open in front of him.

He looked up and smiled his nice smile. I thought he was probably a very happy person. He said, "Miss Perkins is a whiz at conveyancing. Contracts. Copyright. My bag is family law. Less money but more interest, in my humble opinion. So I'm your man, if you want me."

I said, "I don't want to leave home. Can they make me? My parents, I mean. Can you *stop* them?"

An awful thought struck me. Until he mentioned

money I hadn't thought about it. I suppose I must have assumed that going to a solicitor was free, like going to a doctor on the National Health Service. I felt so stupid and ignorant! I thought, *They ought to teach us this sort of thing at school instead of chemistry and math.* (These were my least-favorite subjects.)

I said, "Would it cost a lot?" Then I remembered what the Pag had said when our roof leaked last winter and she was on the phone to the builder. "Could you let me have an estimate?"

"Not absolutely to the last penny," Mr. Twinkle said. "But unless you have a large income we should get legal aid."

He looked at his notebook. "There are things I'd need to know first. Do your mum and dad, or your grandmother, know you are—what shall I say?—seeking the protection of the law? Enterprising of you, in my view, but not everyone would agree with me."

I shook my head. "I don't *talk* to my parents. Not really."

"What about your grandmother?"

This was more difficult. I said, "She won't do anything. I said could we go to law, and she said yes we could but she wouldn't."

Mr. Twinkle nodded. "Well, yes, I suppose your grandmother can hardly be a very young lady, not as young as she used to be, anyway. Quite natural that an older person might find the contemplation of legal action alarming."

Rosie and I both laughed at the idea that the Pag might be frightened of anything, and he looked surprised. I said, "Oh, she's not *scared*. She's not scared of *anything!*"

I thought, *Unless she is scared of her daughter. My mother!*

I said, "She doesn't want us all to quarrel. And I think she thinks they can say things against her."

"Like what?"

I shrugged my shoulders. "Like she's old . . . I don't know. . . ."

He looked at me sharply as if he guessed that wasn't the whole of it. But all he said was, "How long have you lived with your grandmother?"

It would be boring to write down the answers to all his questions—how old I was, how often I saw my mother and father, what did they do for a living, who did I spend my birthdays and Christmas and holidays with, that sort of thing.

In fact, all that stopped it being boring for me in the end was the feeling that behind all these ordinary questions there were other questions lying in wait for me, ones that I preferred not to answer.

I didn't want to tell Mr. Twinkle about the headmaster

calling on the Pag to complain about the way she was bringing me up, feeding me on dog rusks, leaving me alone with her lunatics, frightening nice little boys like William Green, the son of an important man with a title!

The questions stopped suddenly. Mr. Twinkle looked at me, tapping his teeth with the end of his pen. His eyes were crinkled up at the sides, but he was thinking, not smiling. At last he said, "Do you love your grandmother?"

I was embarrassed. Rosie was embarrassed, too. I peeped sideways and saw her cheeks had flamed red. I sighed, but Mr. Twinkle wasn't going to let me off. He had raised an eyebrow and was waiting politely.

I said, crossly, "'Course I do. She's my *relation!*"

"So are your parents," Mr. Twinkle said. "But I don't get the impression that your feelings toward them are loving. Not exactly. Not precisely."

"I don't really like them," I muttered. I couldn't look at him. I knew this was a dreadful thing for anyone to say about her mother and father. Mr. Twinkle would think *I* was dreadful. He would refuse to help me. He would send me away immediately—leap to his feet, shout like thunder, and point to the door. . . .

He said, speaking more slowly and carefully than he had done until now, "Your parents have a right to require you to live with them. If you would prefer to be with someone else, you need what is called a Residence Order to say you must live with that person. Because you are a child, you will have to go to the High Court to ask a judge for permission to apply for this Order. If he agrees, you can go ahead and make the application, and at this stage your parents can object to it."

He stopped and looked at me. "Do you understand?"

"I think so," I said. "I have to go into the witness box and swear to God on the Bible that I want to stay with my grandmother."

I was in no danger of being bored now. This was going to be the most exciting event of my life. I hoped they would give me something to stand on so that I wouldn't look too small and young. I wondered if I should wear my white cashmere sweater or if something dark would be better. I had a dark gray T-shirt from Gap. It was plain but quite smart and perhaps the Pag would lend me the Brooch to pin on the shoulder.

Mr. Twinkle was shaking his head. He said, "I'm sorry to disappoint you, Miss Brooke, but I'm afraid all the swearing will have to be done by me. It is one of the penalties of youth, I fear. The law in its kindly wisdom has decided that people of your age must be spared the trauma of the witness box—and, indeed, the drama of the court altogether in this sort of family matter. You will have to make a statement to me, and eventually the judge may decide he would like to talk to you, but if he does, he will see you in his private room. Without his wig, of course, in case it should frighten you." He was speaking quite gravely, but his eyes were laughing.

"I think that's just stupid," I said. "I wouldn't be a bit frightened!"

"I believe you, Miss Brooke," Mr. Twinkle said. "I can't think that many things frighten you. I am quite sure that you would make a most excellent witness. All the same, before we go any further I would like you to consider talking over what you have decided to do with your grandmother. I think I understand why you want to keep her out of it, and the delicacy of your feelings does you credit. But although no one wants to upset an old lady—"

Rosie interrupted him—suddenly and quite angrily, as if she couldn't bear to keep quiet any longer. "She's not just an *old lady!*"

It was the first time she had spoken. Mr. Twinkle looked startled.

I said, "Shut up, Rosie!"

Rosie said, "I've got to tell him, since you won't. Mr. Twinkle ought to know her name, he ought to know that your grandmother is Dame Halina Lubonirska and a famous person, not what you think of when you call someone an old lady!"

I said, "Don't be snobbish, Rosie. If she weren't a Pag, just an ordinary old person, she'd be just as important."

"That's not what I meant. I meant it wasn't fair to Mr. Twinkle for him not to know. It's kind of cheating. I mean, letting him think you are a poor little girl without a proper grownup to look after you except a helpless old granny without any money. . . ."

I was furious. I said, "I *wasn't* cheating. You are *horrible*, Rosie! I know the Pag isn't helpless but she's got *feelings*, hasn't she? It was *your* mother said she wouldn't want to go to law against her own daughter!"

Mr. Twinkle said, "I have not at any point thought you were trying to cheat me, Miss Brooke. You may have been less than totally open, perhaps, but never deliberately devious. But I'm obliged to you, Rosie. I have indeed heard of Dr. Lubonirska. In fact, I was listening to her on the radio only the other morning, talking about community care for the mentally ill. I imagine, Miss Brooke, that you know your grandmother's views on this subject?"

I looked at my lap, at my fingers twisting together. I peeked sideways at Rosie and knew she was feeling as uncomfortable as I was, ashamed of quarreling in front of a stranger.

Mr. Twinkle said, "Perhaps we should discuss Dr. Lubonirska's views another time. I am right, am I not, to put the stress on the third syllable? Meanwhile, Miss Brooke, perhaps you can tell me why you called your grandmother a Pag? What is a Pag? It is a word I am unfamiliar with."

"Oh, nothing," I mumbled.

But I could see Rosie was starting to smile, and so I

felt bolder and better. I said, "It used to be just a private word, one I made up when I was a baby. But it's come to mean someone who's special in some way. Sort of famous, or powerful. Someone who can make things happen. Like a judge or a policeman . . ."

"Or a solicitor," Rosie said, grinning. Pleased with herself for saying the right thing as usual! Mr. Twinkle was busy writing in his notebook, so I kicked her hard on the ankle.

She yelped and Mr. Twinkle looked up. His eyebrows were raised as if asking a question, but I had the idea that he knew perfectly well what had happened.

He said, "I think Miss Perkins will be finished with Mr. Hornswaddle shortly. It is my turn to make the tea, so perhaps you young ladies would be kind enough to assist me. I *think*—I'm not certain, mind—that we may have a few old mince pies left over from Christmas."

Chapter Ten

THE PAG SAID, "I knew Mr. Twinkle's father. Or was it his grandfather? It was a Twinkle who acted for me when I bought this house. All those years ago!"

The Pag said, "They were Twinkle and Twinkle then. There was no Miss Perkins. But I remember what that office was like. From your description it hasn't changed much."

The Pag said, "I suspect the Twinkles of having tidy minds in spite of the muddle. What looks like mess to one person can be someone else's filing system."

The Pag said, "Smart of you to pick on that particular firm, my clever young friend! Just the right sort of people to ride to the rescue of a damsel in distress."

She was lying on the sofa with Amber curled at her feet and two cats on her lap, smoking an especially noxious French cigarette. She was smiling—one of her Pag-like, secret smiles.

I said, "I thought you'd be angry."

I said, "*You* don't have to do anything. Mr. Twinkle says he can take instructions from me. That means he'll do what I ask him to do."

I said, "It was Rosie's idea in the first place. Her mum said it was the law that they have to listen to children."

I said, "I thought you didn't want *her* to be upset. Your *daughter*! I thought that was why you didn't want to do anything that might mean a quarrel. That's why I didn't tell you."

I said, "I don't want to live with them. I don't want to leave you, and this house, and Amber and Sally and Wilkins. I'd rather die."

I went to bed later than usual that night. The Pag stayed in my room for a long time. When I began to feel sleepy, I told her it was all right, she could go now, but I was glad when she didn't. It felt comfortable and safe to know she was close by, sitting and reading in a soft pool of light.

And that she would be there, if not forever and ever, for as long as she lived, for as long as I needed her.

She was going to talk to Mr. Twinkle in the morning. And to my mother and father.

She had said, "I'll try to persuade them that it's best for you to go on living with me. But if I can't persuade them, then Mr. Twinkle will have to apply for his Residence Order. And then we'll have to march bravely toward the sound of the guns!"

She had laughed, making a joke of it for my sake. She wasn't really looking forward to a battle, I could see. And she didn't want me to be part of it, anyway.

She had said later, when I was in bed and almost asleep, "Listen, young Cat. I won't tell you to put this out of your mind because I know you can't. But try and tell yourself that it's my business now. That you've handed it over to your old Pag of a grandmother and you trust her to sort it out for you!"

Run away and play, little girl, this is serious, grown-up stuff, not something you should worry your pretty head over. . . .

This wasn't what I thought at the time. In fact, *at the time,* I'd been quite glad that the Pag was there and that she had picked up this huge, heavy weight I felt I'd been carting about with me. It was when I was trudging across the common to school the next morning that I suddenly felt myself growing indignant about the way grownups treated people my age as if they were ignorant babies! As if they thought that children's lives were always light and happy, never dark or dangerous.

Even the Pag, who was usually sensible, seemed to think that I should give up thinking about something that was more important to me than to anyone else in the world, and run away to play hopscotch or Pig in the Middle and leave her to do all the worrying.

Off to school, little Cat, back to your sweet, innocent child's life. . . .

I thought, *Has she forgotten about Willy Snotnose and Hairy Ears?* (I checked myself. *No,* I told myself sternly. *William Green. Mr. Baldry.*) Perhaps what happened at school wasn't as important as the things that went on in grown-up Real Life, like wars and famines (or even my mother and father), but it loomed pretty darkly in front of me at this moment. I had managed to keep out of Willy's way *so far,* pretending not to see him by looking *through* him, but Mr. Baldry was another matter.

So much had happened since Sir Archibald Wellington Plunkett Green had stopped that fight between Tom and Willy and marched his sniveling son back into school to make yet another complaint to our headmaster that I had almost forgotten about it. I hadn't been summoned to Mr. Baldry's office yet, but he had been to see the Pag and made it clear he was on Willy's side, so it was only a matter of time.

On the other hand, since he had given the whole

school a long lecture on bullying at the first assembly after the holiday, perhaps individual bullies (like Tom and me, who didn't have titled fathers who were school governors) were to be let off.

I realized that I wasn't bothered about Willy one way or the other. I had been surprised, the first day back at school, to find that I wasn't scared of him any longer. That was partly because of Tom and Rosie. They hadn't *said* anything, but Tom had been sticking close to Rosie and me, waiting at the gate after school and keeping an eye on us in the playground. But now it seemed that it was also because I felt different.

I said to Rosie, "Since half-term, I've felt older and wiser."

That was a daft thing to say, of course. Rosie just laughed, but Tom made a meal of it, staggering helplessly, flapping his arms, and pretending to be seized with awe and amazement. "O Fount of All Wisdom," he cried, kowtowing before me. "O, Great Gray Oracle, Potty Old Prophet, Ancient Seer, how privileged we are to be in your presence."

Rosie hit him on the side of his head with her satchel and said, "Stupid! Girls grow up quicker than boys, it's a known fact."

Tom giggled, but he looked at me quickly to see if he had upset me and I grinned back. I was suddenly feeling enormously cheerful. I wasn't frightened of Willy. I wasn't frightened of Mr. Baldry. I wasn't even afraid of my terrible parents, who didn't seem nearly so terrible now that I knew the Pag was absolutely on my side. She and Mr. Twinkle between them would keep me safe from Lisa and Daddy-O!

I said, "Everything's going to be fine now. I don't know why, I just feel it."

That was a mistake, of course. It's always a mistake to stop watching your back. The moment you think everything is all right is the exact moment when you should start keeping a sharp lookout for trouble.

And on this day, trouble came at the end of the morning.

Our class had been swimming. We were coming back from the pool in the school bus. Rosie and I were sitting in the middle of the back row. The bus had stopped at the school gate and people were jumping up to get their stuff from the racks.

Someone said, "Look, there's Lisa Brooke." A girl's voice, extra shrill, penetrating as a whistle.

People turned. Someone else said, "She's your mum, isn't she, Cat?"

I couldn't see from my place at the back of the bus. I stayed sitting down and pretended to be busy sorting the stuff in my sports bag. I felt hollow inside.

"Let Cat get out quickly, she wants to say hello to her parents."

That was Bossy Fiona, my Spare Tire Friend. "Friend no longer," I growled under my breath.

Someone else said, "Hurry up, Cat! Ask them if they'll give us their autographs."

I shook my head. I wished the ground would open. Rosie spoke urgently into my ear. "They're both there, your mother *and* father, but it's all right, they're getting into a car. Mr. Baldry's saying goodbye to them."

I stood up then. They had made way for me at the window. The car was parked in the playground, in one of the places kept for the staff. My father was already in the driver's seat; I could see his head move as he fastened his seatbelt. My mother was beside the open passenger door, looking up into Mr. Baldry's face and laughing. She was wearing a red cloak and a red beret.

Suddenly, to my immense relief, the doors of the bus closed with a hiss. The driver had stopped the bus in front of the school gates, and he had to move it to let my parents drive out.

I collapsed back into my seat and closed my eyes. I thought hard, concentrating. *Go away, go away, please go away. . . .*

"Did you know they were coming to see the headmaster?"

That was a boy's voice. I opened my eyes. Willy was

straphanging, jerking forward as the bus stopped, its brakes squealing, so that he almost fell on top of me.

I didn't answer him.

He said, "Mr. Baldry told my father that he was going to talk to your parents about your disgusting behavior."

I said, "You stink, William Green. You ought to ask your mother to give you a bath if you can't wash yourself."

Suddenly he looked, and sounded, quite different. He said, "My mother's dead."

I said, "So?" shrugging my shoulders. But his eyes were full of tears and I couldn't go on pretending I didn't care. I thought, *I should have guessed* something! It was always his father who fetched him from school. I said, "I'm sorry."

He said, "Last year," in a choky voice. Then he spoiled it, of course. He blinked and said, "You are hateful, Catriona Brooke, I really do *hate* you!"

And he turned and barged off.

Everyone left the bus except Rosie and me. She said, "I heard what he said. D'you think it's true about his mother?"

Sometimes Rosie quite shocks me. I said, "Oh, Rosie, that's *mean*. No one would lie about a thing like that! You'd be scared it would make it come true."

Rosie pulled a face. But all she said was, "We'd better get off the bus. It's all right, most of them have gone in to lunch. Greedy pigs."

But there were still five or six of them standing around

just inside the gate, some of them giggling, all of them watching me. And we had to walk past them.

Fiona was there. She was waving something.

She said, "Have you seen what they've said about you? I brought the magazine to show you."

Rosie said, "Don't look, Cat. Don't pay attention. Let's just go and have lunch."

She tugged at my arm, but I couldn't move. It was as if my feet were weighed down with lead.

Fiona said, "It's really about your mum and dad, I suppose, but you're in it, too. It's the magazine that comes with the Sunday papers. My mum was wrapping some rubbish this morning and she cut the page out for me."

Two pages, in fact. Several pictures of my mother and father, smiling into the camera or looking at each other. There were pictures of their new house: one of the kitchen, two of the living room, and one of the yellow bedroom I had slept in. And there was a picture of me.

The Pag had taken it in Greece last summer. I was sitting on a stone wall and squinting at the sun. The Pag wasn't much good with a camera, and the photograph was rather dark and a little out of focus.

There were chunks of print between the pictures. I didn't want Fiona to think I was particularly interested, so I read as fast as I could. It was mostly about the hard life my parents had suffered as traveling actors, working the provinces and the seaside resorts, and about how happy they were now, settled in their pretty house and in regular work, famous people at last!

It was all pretty yucky stuff. Embarrassing. But the worst part came at the end. Now these two darling people had their new home, all that was missing was their dear little daughter! My mother had been thinking of me when she painted that yellow bedroom. "Yellow is Catriona's favorite color," she had told the person who had written this article. "I can't wait for her to see it. It will be so wonderful to have her here, at home with us, after all these long years without her."

My favorite color is red, actually. Followed by blue. Yellow comes a very long way down my list of preferences. Not that it mattered. Not beside the awful headline at the top of the article. *Successful Television Star Longs for Her Daughter. Says Lisa Brooke, "I cannot be happy until my little family is whole again."*

I felt hot and cold. I felt sick. I couldn't look at anyone.

Rosie said in a scornful voice, "What a load of rubbish they write! My mother won't allow this sort of cheap magazine in the house. She says only common people read them."

I knew that Rosie's mother would never say a mean thing like that. All the same, I was grateful to Rosie. She had made me brave enough to say, "It's rubbish, of course, but can I keep it, Fiona? Just to show to my grandmother. It's against the law to write lies about people in the newspaper. I expect my grandmother will want to instruct our solicitor."

Fiona looked at me blankly. I said kindly, "That's what you say when you tell your solicitor to go to law. You say, 'I am going to instruct my solicitor.'"

I sneaked a look at Rosie and saw her cheeks were growing fatter, a sure sign that she was about to collapse with one of her giggling fits, so I looked at my watch and said quickly, "There won't be any lunch left if we don't hurry. I'll give you the article back tomorrow, Fiona."

And I set off at a smart trot, Rosie behind me. She was bursting to laugh but didn't explode until we were in the dining room, in the line for the hatch, and no one near us would know what she was laughing at.

By then, I wasn't sure it was so funny. I had actually been rather foul to Fiona, mocking her for not knowing what "instruct a solicitor" meant. But why should she have known? Unless their father is some kind of criminal, a burglar or a mugger, very few people of twelve have much to do with the law.

"I'm sorry to laugh," Rosie said. "I couldn't help it. Are you really going to show that magazine thing to your grandmother? Is it true about your mother and father?"

"I don't know." I looked at the hamburger on the plate I had just picked up from the hatch and thought I should be sick if I tried to eat it. I said, "I hope it isn't."

I looked at Rosie and she looked at me. She wasn't laughing now, and neither was I. Each of us knew what the other was thinking.

Because I didn't want to live with my parents, I didn't want to be told that they wanted me.

I said, "Perhaps I could just cut off a bit of me. A leg, or an arm. Would that fix it?"

"You'd have to send it by registered post," Rosie said. "But it would have to stop bleeding first. You could put it in the freezer overnight, that should do it."

"Wouldn't it start bleeding again soon as it unfroze? Leak out of the parcel?"

Rosie screwed up her eyes, pretending to be deep in scientific thought. "I don't think so. I think you only go on bleeding as long as your heart's pumping through the whole of your body. I'll have to ask Mum."

"Perhaps she'd chop the bit off for me, it would be more hygienic," I said. I did my best to laugh. But my stomach felt fluttery.

I said, "It's not really so funny."

Rosie shook her head. She whispered, "Don't cry, Cat, not here where they can see you."

It was her mouth, not mine, that had started to quiver. She said, "Oh, Cat, I'm so sorry."

Chapter Eleven

THE PAG SAID, "What else could your mother say? That she hadn't missed you much all these years?"

I was surprised. I hadn't expected the Pag to burst into tears when she read the magazine article, but I'd thought it might make her just a little bit sad to think of her only daughter being lonely for *her* only daughter.

Instead, she was smiling.

I said, "You mean she was lying? That's a mean thing to say."

"Not lying," the Pag said. "I'm sure she meant what she said when she said it. She usually does."

I said, "She got a bedroom ready for me. Painted yellow."

"A useful color. Nice and bright and sunny," the Pag said.

"You mean she might not have meant it for me? Not altogether?"

"I wouldn't say that," the Pag said.

"Yellow isn't my favorite color."

"No. *I* know it isn't," the Pag said.

"That's not *her* fault, is it? You knowing me better."

The Pag nodded. I wasn't sure what she was thinking.

I said, "She dumped me, though, didn't she? And she wasn't to know I'd be happier here than with her."

"You don't have to be angry with her," the Pag said. "Nor sorry for her. Anger and pity are things to keep clear of when you need to make up your mind."

I said, "What d'you mean? I've made up my mind. You know that."

We were sitting in the kitchen. The Pag had the magazine article spread out on the table in front of her. She folded it slowly. She said, "I won't argue with you. I'm a selfish old woman."

I thought I knew what she meant, but I had to be sure. I said, "You mean you want me to stay with you? Because you love me more than her even though she's your only daughter?"

"That's just about it, my young friend," the Pag said, and looked at me grimly.

It is always surprising in life, the way things never turn

out to be what you expected. I thought the High Court would be a flat-faced building made of glass, like a huge bank. Instead, there was this palace of white stone, full of towers and twiddly bits, like a fairy-tale castle.

"Disneyland," I said to the Pag, while we stood outside waiting for Mr. Twinkle.

She was wearing the Brooch on a new black jacket and looked unusually smart. I was wearing my school uniform because I was going straight to school after we had been to the judge. I had wanted to take the day off so I could wear ordinary clothes, but the Pag thought the judge would be more impressed if I wore my uniform. "He'll see I'm a responsible guardian for you, putting education before idle amusement," she said. It was a joke, but I could see she half meant it. And she had made me polish my shoes before we left, and sent me to the bathroom to clean my teeth *twice*.

A taxi stopped and Mr. Twinkle got out—though "got out" sounds too ordinary for what seemed to happen. He had to bend almost double to get through the door, holding on to the big black hat he was wearing, and then he *unfolded* himself, very slowly and gradually, like a tall, thin plant growing in a speeded-up nature film, until he was twice the height of just about everyone else walking by on the pavement. He even made the Pag look small.

He touched the curly brim of his hat and looked down at us from the lofty heights that he lived in. "Oh dear," he said, "I have kept you waiting. I don't think I'm late by the clock, but I am certainly late by good manners, I must beg you both to forgive me."

The Pag said that was all right, we had arrived much too early, and he gave us one of his big, beaming smiles.

"Forward then," he said. "I must warn you it's rather a case of 'Oh my fur and whiskers' once you get inside."

I knew what he meant about half an hour later. Inside the High Court was a maze of dark corridors, turrets, and twisty stone stairs. A rabbit warren. A man in a black gown told us to follow him and we scuttled in and out, and up and down, and roundabout, for what seemed like ages. And when we got to wherever it was we were going, and the man turned to leave us, I saw his bulgy eyes and his little nose twitching.

I tugged at Mr. Twinkle's sleeve. I said, "*Alice in Wonderland.*"

"A general statement, Miss Brooke," Mr. Twinkle said. "No reference to any particular rabbity fellow. Just a piece of advice. Regard your encounter with the law as an excursion to Wonderland and you won't come to much harm. Your grandmother and I are going to have a chat with the judge now. You wait here, on this bench, and we'll be back in a jiffy. I'm sorry. Correction. 'Several jiffies' would be more accurate. The judge may want a word with you, he may not. Don't worry about it. This is the easy bit."

In television programs, going to law is exciting. The judge sits high above the court, wearing a wig and a robe. He is always quite old. He asks clever questions, and you get the feeling he thinks he knows more than anyone else in the world. He is often rude to the other lawyers, even though they are wearing wigs, too, but he is usually polite to the jury who have to decide at the end whether the prisoner in the dock is guilty or innocent. However hard he tries, the judge can't make the jury say that the person on trial is guilty when they think he is innocent.

In real life (unless, I suppose, you are on trial for something like murder) going to law is not as exciting as it is on the telly. The trouble is, such a lot of what goes on is so boring. Hours and hours of just waiting. Hanging around drafty corridors. Sitting on benches . . .

I sat on that bench for what felt like a year. My bottom got numb and I felt myself falling asleep. Suddenly, the rabbity man in the black gown was there. He said, "The judge would like to see you now, Miss Brooke. Please follow me."

He whisked away round a corner. I ran after him, my heart suddenly thumping with excitement and terror. I said, under my breath, "Oh my fur and whiskers!"

But there was nothing to be excited by, or afraid of.

The judge was so ordinary. No wig, no gown—just a little man with a sweet, wrinkled face and bright button eyes like a very old mouse. He was sitting on a gold throne in a tiny round room in a turret with an enormous tin of chocolate biscuits open on a gold stool in front of him. He nodded at me and pushed the tin toward me.

If I had thought he had put the biscuits there just for me, because I was a child, I wouldn't have taken one. But he was munching away himself, and there were crumbs on his lap and flecks of chocolate on his tie.

I wasn't sure what to call him. In television films a judge is *My Lord* or *Your Lordship*, but it seemed silly to call him that when we were sitting eating chocolate biscuits together. So I just said, "Thank you, sir."

He brushed his hands together to get rid of the crumbs. He said, "I hope you are as fond of chocolate as I am. Only dark chocolate, mind. Can't abide milk, wishy-washy stuff, no bite to it. Maybe that's just an old person's taste. Or maybe not. Always prepared to admit I am wrong. What about your grandmother?"

"She doesn't eat chocolate at all," I said. "But that's because she smokes. It turns you off sweet things. It's one good reason not to smoke if you like chocolate."

He bobbed his head up and down like a bird drinking. He said, "There are other reasons for not smoking. But you know that. Your grandmother will have told you." He cocked his head on one side. "Do you like jokes? My grandson told me a good one the other day. Why did the dinosaur cross the road?"

I said, "Because they hadn't invented chickens yet." I thought for a second that he looked at me sadly, but then he stood up, smiled his sweet-mouse smile, and said, "Thank you for talking to me, Catriona," in a suddenly superior and gracious way, almost as if he were royalty. I remembered when the Pag went to the Palace to be made a Dame, she had to curtsey to the Queen, and I knew I should do something like that, curtsey or walk backward, to show respect. I stepped back. And fell over. And woke up.

I was still on the bench. The Pag and Mr. Twinkle were standing in front of me. I said, "I was dreaming I saw the judge."

"Busy fellow," Mr. Twinkle said. "Time to make an appearance in a young lady's dream but got rid of us in a twinkling. Sorry. Bad pun. On to the next stage. Steady the Buffs!"

I said to the Pag in the train going home, "What did he mean, 'Steady the Buffs'?"

The Pag said, "There was a surgeon I knew when I first came to England who used to say 'Steady the Buffs' when the aid raid sirens went and we had to move some of the patients to the hospital basement. I asked him what it meant—a lot of English idiom seemed very strange to me at that time—and he said the Buffs were the old Third Regiment of the Line. I suppose keeping steady was how they won battles. What Mr. Twinkle meant is that we're through the first stage but we've a long way to go."

"I can keep *steady*. It's just a bit boring. I thought going to the High Court would be much more exciting."

The Pag sighed, a small sigh. She said, "That's why he said 'Steady the Buffs.' Not 'Charge into battle.' There are times when steady and boring is best."

The Pag didn't often go on in this dull grown-up way. I thought she must be feeling tired, or ill. I said, "'Cheer up for Chatham, Dover's in sight,' that's what Tom's teacher says, and I bet you don't know where it comes from. I don't suppose Mr. Muckleberry knows either, and he's the one always says it. But you can tell what it means all right, can't you?"

She started to smile, I was glad to see. She said, "As long as you remember there may be 'Rapids Ahead.' I think, though I'm not sure, that is a Canadian boating song."

And she laughed. And I laughed. Which we wouldn't have done if we had known what was lying in wait for us.

Chapter Twelve

THE PAG GOT THE LETTER by the morning post after I had gone to school. So I had no forewarning.

Our class went to the sports center for swimming that afternoon and I won my Lifesaving Badge. I was the first person in our class to get one this term, and it made me so cheerful I sang all the way home.

I couldn't wait to tell the Pag. I shouted "Guess what!" as I unlocked the front door and skidded into the hall. . . .

And then I stopped dead.

The Pag was standing center stage—in the exact middle of the grubby old rug on which the dogs and the cats deposit mud and melting snow and sometimes dead birds when they come in through the front door. She was usually in her study when I came home from school. She didn't stop working (so she said) until she heard the barbarians at the gate. (The barbarians were me, and sometimes Rosie and Tom.)

It wasn't finding her in the wrong place that drove the Lifesaving Badge out of my head. It was the look on her face.

She was smiling, but it was a queer, cold, fixed smile, as if someone had stitched the corners of her mouth upward and shoved her head in the freezer.

She said, "You're home early."

"I *ran*," I said. "I ran across the common and caught the first train. Rosie couldn't keep up and she missed it."

"Oh," she said. "Well."

She put her finger to her lip and tipped her head in the direction of the living room, and I assumed that one of her patients was waiting there. So when she whispered, "Come and help me make tea," I said, "I'll do it for you. Shall I bring it in on a tray or just call you to fetch it?" (Some of her funny old people liked to see me. Others didn't.)

But she followed me into the kitchen and closed the door. She stood with her back against it and said, "Someone wants to talk to you. There was a letter this morning and I rang the office at once. I thought I might sort it out before you came home. . . ." She stopped, then said angrily, "But you had to be early!"

I stared at her. It could have been someone else speaking. She must have realized it herself because she gave a sudden shy laugh as a kind of apology. She said, "It's nothing you need worry about."

I said, "What's *it*? And who's *someone*?"

"I'm sorry, Cat," she said. I watched her while she changed back from the old and dithery person she had so strangely become to her normal Pag-self. It was weird. I wondered if everyone had several different people inside them, even though most of the time they only used one.

The Pag, the Pag I was used to, anyway, said in her normal crisp voice, "There is a social worker sitting in our living room. She is quite harmless and slightly alarmed at the moment because Tredegar decided to bring her a dead mouse as a gift the moment she sat down on the sofa. If she could see you and reassure herself that you are healthy and well and suitably cared for, I think she would be happy to leave very soon."

Tredegar was our big black tom, who brought in most of the dead mice and birds, as well as a gray squirrel occasionally.

I said, "What's she *doing* here? This social work person. Is it my fault? Because I don't want to live with my mother and father?"

The Pag shook her head. "I don't think that comes into it. Apparently, someone has tipped off the Social

Services, suggested that you may be neglected. Starved, beaten, that sort of thing. We know you are not, but they don't know, do they? And of course it is good to know that our children are so carefully watched over."

"Liar! You don't mean that, do you? You mean just the opposite!"

She ignored this. She said, "I think it would be a kindness if you would present yourself in the living room. You could at least rescue the poor woman from Tredegar."

"D'you mean you left her *alone*, with him swearing at her?"

"I'm afraid so." She didn't sound in the least sorry.

The social worker was huddled at one end of the sofa and Tredegar crouched at her feet. He was growling savagely and drooling over the present he had brought her. It was a very large dead mouse. Big enough to be a dead rat.

She turned her head as I came in—just a small movement, but Tredegar snarled louder, hunching his shoulders and swaying his hips as if preparing to spring on her. She gave a faint moan and closed her eyes.

I said, "Tredder, you *beast*," and picked up the mouse and put it out of his reach in the corner cupboard where the Pag keeps the drinks and the glasses. He gave another growl, more piteous than menacing, and slunk away to hide under the bookcase.

I said, "His bark is worse than his bite. They say that about dogs but it can be true of cats, too."

She opened her eyes and looked around fearfully. "Has he gone?"

"Under the bookcase." She was looking so silly and scared that I couldn't help adding, "He'll probably stay there as long as I'm in the room. He just isn't accustomed to strangers."

"Then perhaps you'll stay and protect me." She smiled, a friendly smile, if a bit nervous. She said, "My name is Gloria. You must be Catriona."

I wanted to say I was used to being called Miss Brooke by people like lawyers and social workers, but I thought the Pag would be upset if I was cheeky. So I just nodded.

Gloria looked at me and I looked at her. She said, "Come and sit down. Did your grandmother explain why I'm here?"

I said, "Someone told lies about us. Saying she starved me and kept me locked up in the attic."

She grinned—almost giggled. When she smiled, she was quite young and pretty. Then she sat up and became a different person, just as the Pag had done in the kitchen. She said, "What nonsense, of course not!"

I said, "What did they say, then? And *who* said it?"

Gloria said, "Let's just say there has been some concern about you."

She was putting on a posh voice as if to make sure I

understood that I was only a child and had no right to ask questions. So I said nothing, and that seemed to be what she wanted because she gave a satisfied little nod and then smiled at me kindly.

She said, "Your mother and father are such lovely actors. I always watch their program. I expect you do, too. And I'm told they are charming to meet in real life."

"Who told you that?" I asked, although I knew the answer. She didn't answer, so I went on, "Was it my headmaster? No one else round here knows them. They live miles away, the other side of London, in Surrey. But they went to see *him*. Mr. Baldry. They want to take me away from my grandmother."

"I don't know anything about that," Gloria said. She looked at me quickly—and decided to be honest. "I mean, it isn't my job to interfere in the arrangements your family make for you, as long as I'm sure you are properly cared for."

She was glancing round the room, frowning a little, as if she was checking for cobwebs and dust. I realized that White Queen, the oldest of all the cats, had been on the sofa again and had shed a great many long, white hairs. And Gloria was wearing dark trousers and a blue blazer.

"I eat a lot," I said. "My grandmother cooks me huge breakfasts. This morning I had three eggs and five slices of toast."

Gloria looked at me. I wished I was fatter. I sat up

straight and puffed my chest out. I said, "I'm a naturally thin person. I can eat and *eat* like ten thousand *horses* but it doesn't make any difference."

Gloria said, "It must be quite hard work for your granny, looking after a big, growing girl."

"I look after her, too," I said. "We look after each other."

"Your granny still goes out to work, doesn't she?"

I couldn't tell if this was a bad thing or a good thing. If going out meant leaving me alone, that was bad. On the other hand, going out to work in a lady her age, must be good. Better than sleeping in front of the television all day like Fiona's granny, who had varicose veins and drove Fiona's mother wild.

I said cautiously, "She goes to give lectures. And sometimes she talks on the radio. But she's at home mostly, writing her book."

"Oh, I know Dr. Lubonirska has retired from the Health Service," Gloria said. "But she still sees a few patients at home, is that right?"

"Not often," I said. "And usually when I'm at school. I think that's rather a pity because I want to be a doctor when I grow up and it's a good idea to have a bit of practice. Though none of them are really ill, no more than you and me, just a bit old and lonely and sad."

It is very easy to tell lies once you start. Easier than telling the truth in a good many ways. Although what I had just told Gloria didn't feel like a lie, except the bit about wanting to be a doctor. Perhaps one of the other people inside me had changed her mind about that!

Anyway, Gloria seemed to believe me. She asked me some more questions—about my favorite subjects at school, and what kind of television programs I liked to watch, and who were my friends, and did I get on with the other children at school. All these questions were simple to answer, even the last one. I said, in case she knew about William Green, that there was one boy in my class who was a bit of a bully, but we were friends now. I looked her straight in the eye as I said it, and she seemed to believe me.

She started fussing about round her feet, looking for her handbag and another bigger bag she had with her. She said, "I'll just have a quick word with your granny and then I'll be off." She started to get up and stopped. "Is it safe? Or will that nasty brute go for me?"

"Not while I'm here," I said coldly. If she hadn't called Tredegar a brute, I might have warned her about the white hairs on her back and her bottom. I hoped the Pag wouldn't notice.

I listened at the living room door while she and the Pag said goodbye in the hall but the Pag didn't mention White Queen. It was Gloria who did all the talking, saying how interesting it had been to meet Dr. Lubonirska, how she hoped she had not taken up too much time but she hoped Dr. Lubonirska would understand. . . .

The Pag murmured something too low for me to hear. The front door opened. Gloria said, "Cheery-bye." And the front door closed.

The Pag laughed. I looked at her, standing there in the hall, her arms wrapped round herself, laughing.

I said, "Did you see? All those white hairs? Why didn't you tell her?"

"Revenge," the Pag said. "Not that it was her fault. She was just doing her job, as they say."

I said, "She can't *do* anything, can she?"

The Pag shook her head.

I said, "It's awful. People like that walking into other people's houses and asking all these rude questions. Like a policeman. As if we were criminals."

"If you'd really been starved or locked up, you might have been glad to see her," the Pag said.

"*Was* it Mr. Baldry who told them I was?"

The Pag hunched her shoulders and spread out her hands, palms upward, in the way she did sometimes. It made her look foreign.

I said, "I expect Willy's horrible father had something to do with it. I'd like to *kill* him."

"Is that steam I can see coming out of your ears?" the Pag said.

I said, "*You* were angry too!"

"I'm ashamed of it," the Pag said. "That's the difference between your age and mine."

I thought she looked dreadfully tired all of a sudden. I thought, *It's me, I'm a nuisance.* But then she smiled, crinkling her eyes, and put her hand on my shoulder, and said, "I think we've got something to celebrate, haven't we? I thought when you came in, *She's got something to tell me.*"

Chapter Thirteen

WE WENT OUT TO DINNER at the Italian restaurant round the corner from Perkins and Twinkle to celebrate my Lifesaving Badge, and the Pag said she would write a note to excuse me from my math homework.

"A headache," she said.

"That's a lie," I said, stuffing my mouth with spaghetti.

"Sometimes the truth is too complicated."

"It's true that I couldn't face algebra homework this evening. But then I've always hated algebra, anyway."

"There you are," the Pag said. "What would be the point in muddying the clear statement of the first sentence with a qualification in the second? Or to put it more simply, it is a waste of everyone's time for me to write and say we had a visit from the Social Services that upset you sufficiently to make it hard to work on a subject you already find difficult."

"That's too long a sentence," I said. "You'll run out of puff. And it's still telling a lie to say I had a headache."

"All right," the Pag said. "But it is I who am telling the lie, so it need not trouble your conscience. All you have to do is concentrate your intellectual effort on which ice cream you fancy."

"Vanilla and strawberry and chocolate. I don't need to think about it. Are you having an ice cream? Or are you going to *smoke?*"

I spat out this last word with as much contempt as anyone can manage while eating spaghetti with tomato sauce.

"I don't want an ice cream," the Pag said. "But I won't have a cigarette, in case it spoils your pleasure."

"That's not fair," I said. "Putting *me* in the wrong when it ought to be you."

This was a game we played, pretending to quarrel, and the person who lost was the one who laughed first. Like all private games it didn't seem as funny to other people as it seemed to us and I suddenly realized that someone was watching and listening.

A little girl, six or seven, sitting at a table on the other side of the room, was staring solemnly at us. She was pretty, with big gray eyes and dark lashes, but her long hair looked greasy and tangly as if it hadn't been washed or brushed for ages, and her pink anorak was dirty. She was alone at the table.

I wondered where her mother was and decided that she was probably in the lavatory. The little girl didn't look frightened, being left on her own. But I smiled at her all the same, just in case.

She smiled back. I said, "Where's Mummy?" and her gray eyes grew bigger and rounder as if I had said something to frighten her. Then she looked past me, toward the back of the restaurant. I turned my head and saw Willy coming out of the men's toilets with his father behind him.

I felt as if I were falling through space. My ears were buzzing. I whispered, "Pag . . ." and she looked up.

I saw from her face that she recognized Willy. So she would have guessed that the tall man behind him must be his father. And Willy knew her, of course. It would be difficult to forget the Pag once you'd seen her. But Sir Archibald Wellington Plunkett Green wouldn't know the Pag was the person who had threatened to throw his precious son into the middle of next week.

Unless—or until—he recognized me.

I tried to shrink myself small. I stared at the menu as if my life depended on learning the list of ice creams by heart. I thought of all the stories I had read when I was younger about people who could make themselves invisible whenever they wanted. But you needed a magic ring. Or a spell.

It seemed as if the restaurant had fallen silent around me. *Everyone must be staring*, I thought. The Pag said, "Cat," in a warning voice. She spoke softly, but it was like a shout in my ears.

I knew I had to look at Willy. I unfocused my eyes so that he looked blurred and swimmy. All the same, I could see he was pulling a face, wrinkling his nose and screwing his mouth up as if he smelled something bad. He whispered something to the small girl beside him that made her giggle and put her hand over her mouth.

Sir Archibald Wellington Plunkett Green was reading the menu. I twisted in my chair so that if he glanced in my direction he would only see the back of my head.

I looked despairingly at the Pag. She mouthed, "Steady the Buffs," at me, to try and make me smile, but all I wanted to do was shrivel up and die.

The waiter had taken my spaghetti plate away and brought a glass dish of ice cream. The ice cream in this restaurant was better than any ice cream I had ever tasted, but at this moment, even though I had picked up the spoon, I felt I should be sick if I ate it.

Sir Archibald Wellington Plunkett Green suddenly cleared his throat loudly, and I dropped my spoon. It bounced once on the table and fell on the floor with a clatter.

Willy snorted with laughter. He was writhing around in his chair, rolling his eyes and clutching his stomach, as if a person dropping her spoon was the funniest thing he had ever seen in his whole life.

Sir Archibald Wellington Plunkett Green said, "Behave yourself, William. You're a boy, not a gorilla."

The small girl said, "Gorillas are nicer than William. I'd rather have a gorilla for a brother than him."

Sir Archibald laughed. The waiter brought me another spoon and I had to look up at him to say thank you, which meant I had to turn round in my chair. And once I'd done that, I couldn't just stare straight in front of me, so I looked sideways, at Willy's table.

They were all looking at me. Willy's father was watching me over his spectacles, which were slipping down his thin nose. He had gray eyes like Willy. And like Willy's sister.

Everyone seemed to be waiting for me to do something. I said, "Hello, Willy."

The Pag smiled at me encouragingly.

I said, "The spaghetti is excellent. You can have it with tomato sauce, or with sauce bolognese. And they make their own ice cream. And that's excellent, too."

"Thank you," Sir Archibald said. "That's very helpful. My daughter will be particularly grateful to know about the ice cream."

He looked at the Pag and bowed his head slightly. His

gray eyes had gone cold. I heard Willy catch his breath. He looked at his father, then at the Pag, then at me. Wondering what was going to happen. Excited, and scared.

I knew what he was feeling because I felt the same way myself. I heard Fat Boy's voice in my head. *Your dad's a Pag, come to that, Willy.* Pags were powerful people. That's what I'd told Fat Boy and Willy and Fish Breath when they had chased me on the train. I'd made it up because I had been afraid they were going to kill me, but it was true that the Pag, *my* Pag, was different from most people's grand-mothers, and Willy's father was a school governor and a knight.

If they'd both been knights in the olden days they would have charged each other on horseback. Or if they'd been a witch and a warlock, they could have had a com-petition to see who could cast the strongest spell. But it was hard to see what they could do nowadays, except per-haps shout at each other.

The Pag didn't shout. She said in a quiet, smiley voice, "I hope you're feeling better now, Willy. Catriona told me you were ill before Christmas."

"I had an operation in hospital," Willy said. He looked slyly sideways at me, a bit relieved, a bit disappointed. Then he looked at his father and whispered in an awed, husky voice, "Cat's granny has got a real Harley-Davidson. And she used to have a Vincent Black Shadow."

His father raised his eyebrows and smiled at the Pag. "Fame," he said. "Your place in my son's pantheon is assured, I think."

The Pag said, "It's a beautiful bike. If you're interested in bikes, you must come and look at it, Willy."

I was jealous. I said, "I ride pillion. Once we went all the way to Greece and back. It's really *fabulous*. You just can't *believe* . . ."

I rolled my eyes and sighed to show that no words could express the wonder of being a passenger on a Harley-Davidson, even though I wasn't really all that keen on biking talk or on biking long distances. The Pag had all the fun of doing the driving, and the helmet gave me a headache and mussed up my hair so that it took ages to get out the tangles. The Pag had suggested I go to the hairdresser and have it cut short, but Rosie and I had promised each other to grow our hair right down to our bottoms, and so the Pag had brushed and brushed and made me two long, shiny plaits every night.

I knew now that Willy hadn't been lying when he said his mother was dead. If she had been alive, his little sister's hair would have been cleaner and tidier. She was at the age when long hair is too difficult to take care of yourself, but you can't bear a stranger to brush it.

I wondered how I would feel if my mother was dead. When Rosie and I were about five years old, at primary school, a boy called Ben had come to school one Monday morning with a black band on the arm of his jacket because his mother had died. He boasted about his armband until everyone in the class wanted one. But Willy's little sister was older than we had been then.

Her name was Mary. She was laughing at something the Pag must have said to her while I had been eating my ice cream and thinking.

"My middle name is Mary," the Pag said, telling her something *I* didn't know.

She had paid the bill. She looked at me inquiringly and I nodded firmly. Politeness was one thing but getting too friendly was quite another.

"You never told *me* that," I said crossly as we came out into the cold black night and the wind.

The Pag tucked her hand under my elbow. "It was never important. Only just now, it was something to say to a child who seemed lonely to me."

"Her mother's dead," I said. "She died last year. Rosie thought Willy might be making it up or I would have told you."

She squeezed my arm. "He must miss his mother. You said he was younger than the other boys in his gang. Perhaps he fell into bad company."

I said, "I don't see why you should stick up for him. Making excuses."

She was quiet for a while. When we turned out of the High Street the roads were empty, and our footsteps echoed. At last she said, "It's only a week or two until the case comes up. The judge will expect to see a school report. Your parents have been to see Mr. Baldry, and Willy's father has your headmaster's ear."

I said, "But Willy's father doesn't know anything about me. Almost *nothing*."

"Things add up," the Pag said. "Until this is over and settled, we have to watch our P's and Q's, you and I. We need friends, not enemies."

I began to see enemies all around me. I tried to be good at school, not answering back, or reading under my desk when I was bored, or cheating in math lessons by getting Rosie to smuggle the answers across the aisle to me. I tried to think before I spoke, and use my knife and fork properly, and never talk with my mouth full, and I didn't once shout or sing in the train going home. I tried to be neat and good and helpful to everyone, and it was a terrible strain.

It was a strain until Thursday, when something much more terrible took my mind off it. At the end of assembly, Mr. Baldry announced that he had something very important to tell the whole school and we must pay especial attention, by which he meant not merely no shuffling or whispering but alert, alive minds in full listening mode. (This is our headmaster's style. It was not meant as a joke.)

And there was nothing to joke about. At half-term, two fifteen-year-old boys had broken into an old lady's bungalow and stolen her handbag and jewelry. A neighbor had heard breaking glass, and they had been caught by the police as they ran away. But the police had not been in time to save the old lady. Before the boys robbed her, they had tied her up in her armchair and set fire to her hair.

There was a booming sound in my head, and the headmaster's voice seemed to be coming from the other end of a long tunnel. Although the old lady was still alive, she was very ill in the hospital. The boys had been in custody ever since. And one of them was a boy from our school.

Mr. Baldry went on for a long time about how shocked he had been that a boy who had been given the amazing privilege of being educated at our school could do something so wicked. It was an appalling stain on the honor of the school, and we must all do our best to atone for it. We must pray for the sinners. Especially for our fellow student Saul Fisher.

It took me several seconds to realize that Saul Fisher was Fish Breath. A girl somewhere behind me started to wail and several girls in my form were crying. Rosie, who was sitting next to me, tugged at my hand. She whispered, "Look at Willy."

He was at the end of our row. He was swaying, and deathly white.

"He's going to faint," Rosie said. "Someone ought to do something."

But before he crumpled to the floor, Mrs. Morgan, our class teacher, had her arm around him, supporting him. I heard her say quite loudly and clearly to another teacher standing beside her, "He ought to have his head examined, upsetting the young ones," and I knew she was so angry with Mr. Baldry that she didn't care who heard her.

After assembly we had Mrs. Morgan for two English periods. Instead of dictation and spelling she read us *Little Lord Fauntleroy* because she said what we all needed "after that" was a nice story with a happy ending, and since it had recently been on television, even those of us who didn't like reading might enjoy listening.

I had just finished reading it to myself for about the fourth time, and although I was happy to listen to Mrs. Morgan with part of my mind, I spent a lot of the morning trying to make Willy look at me. He was sitting about four desks away and if he had looked up at all he must have seen me. But he sat gazing down at his two hands clasped on top of his desk all the time Mrs. Morgan was reading.

He couldn't have known about Fish Breath until the assembly. He looked pale and ill, as if he had been shocked out of his mind. When the bell went for break he lifted his head and started to cry. He cried like a baby, dribbling and sniveling, the tears streaming down. Mrs.

Morgan put down her book and went to him. She sat on his desk and held him, hiding his face against her, while the rest of the class left the room. A few people were sniggering uncomfortably, but most of us were quiet and shy with one another. It was hard to know what to say about what had happened, even to your best friend.

Rosie said, in the playground, "Are you going to tell Mrs. Morgan?"

"I don't know." I didn't want to decide about anything.

Rosie said, "Was it *him* all the time? Fish Breath? His gang, not Willy's?"

I wondered if she thought it was all right to call him Fish Breath now we knew that he was a criminal.

I said, "It was Fish Breath tried to set fire to my hair. But I don't know about telling on Willy. The Pag says Willy got into bad company because his mother was dead. I suppose you'd call Fish Breath bad company."

"Willy's younger than the others," Rosie said. "Perhaps they wanted him in the gang because he's strong. He could take the blame for things and nothing much would happen since he's only twelve. Like people taking little kids along when they go shoplifting."

Sometimes the things Rosie pretends to know really amaze me. I said, "You mean they took Willy thieving?"

Rosie gave one of her sighs. "It was just an example," she said. "Just to explain that someone ought to know

Willy's been mixed up with that lot. Before they make him do something awful."

I felt heavy and miserable. I didn't want to tell anyone anything. I had tried to tell Mr. Baldry and he had blamed me. Anything I told anyone was bound to go wrong.

Rosie said, "I suppose you could tell your grandmother."

She sounded impatient, as if this was the very last thing any normal person would think of, but I felt as if a great weight had been lifted. Of course the Pag would know what to do!

Rosie said, in a surprised voice, "What are you grinning for?"

"Nothing," I said.

We had French next, then history. I kept looking at the clock above the blackboard, and the hands moved so slowly I thought several times that the clock must have stopped. I stuffed my hands between my knees because they felt trembly and tried not to think about the old woman, about her hair burning. If she was very old, perhaps she had thin gray hair, like Rosie's grandmother. I saw Rosie's grandmother sitting in her armchair by the window, a gag in her mouth and her hands tied behind her, and her hair crackling. I wanted to cry.

I wanted the Pag.

The morning was nearly over. We had art all afternoon, and sometimes we finished art lessons early and managed to catch an earlier train. I thought of myself running home from the station, throwing open the gate, hurtling through the front door. And the Pag would be waiting.

But it didn't work out like that. Before lunch, I was kidnapped by my father.

Chapter Fourteen

PARENTS WHO TURNED UP at lunchtime were either fussy or doting. The fussy ones brought extra sweaters and gloves if the weather had turned cold. The doting ones came with homework their treasures had forgotten to take with them, or bags of crisps or sweets in case their precious darlings should faint with hunger before the bell went for school lunch.

Neither the Pag nor Rosie's mum was a doter or a fusser, so we never expected to see them at the school gate at the end of the morning; if we looked to see who was there, it was only to spy out who were the spoiled brats in our class.

I might have missed Daddy-O if he hadn't called out

to me. He was sitting in the car with the window down. He was waving and grinning.

I was *shocked rigid*. That is, so deeply embarrassed at the idea of being seen with him that when he said, "Hop in, kiddo," I ducked my head and scrambled into the passenger seat without even looking at Rosie.

And I was relieved when he started the car and drove round the corner, out of sight of the playground and of the various doters and fussers, eyes out on stalks as they recognized the heartthrob of *The Waiting Room*.

It wasn't until we were in the fast lane of the dual carriageway that I began to have doubts. He was whistling through his teeth and driving like Jehu. (Jehu is a charioteer in the Bible who "driveth furiously," in case you don't know.) I wanted to tell him to go slower, but then I remembered how my mother screeched about his driving. So I said, "I haven't had lunch yet."

"Oh, we'll have lunch."

He didn't look at me. (He was going so fast that was just as well!)

I said, "It's been paid for. The school lunch."

This was a silly thing to say. He didn't answer it. I said, "Where are we going?"

"Lunch first, obviously. Since you appear to be hungry."

I said, "I'm not starving. Not greedy-hungry. It's just, we're not supposed to go out at lunchtime without asking permission, and afternoon school starts at two o'clock."

He said nothing.

I said, "It's art this afternoon."

"It won't hurt you to miss art."

It was then I began to be frightened. Not badly frightened, not stomach-turning, just queasy. I said, "What's the big idea?" Trying to sound as if I thought it was all a bit of a joke.

He said, "I thought we should have a talk. Before this thing comes to court."

"You didn't have to *kidnap* me. Not just so's we could *have a talk!*" I sneered, turning the corners of my mouth down and flaring my nostrils. But he wasn't watching.

He was smiling a little. He said, "It seemed the only way to get you alone. Without your mother interfering. Or your grandmother."

"*She* doesn't interfere," I said. "She's not trying to take me away from my home. That's you and Lisa."

I was angry, and I wanted to sound angry. But my voice wobbled.

"It's what Lisa wants," he said. "What your mother wants. Not what I want, necessarily. Or not first and foremost."

We had turned off the main road and were driving along a lane, trees and hedges on either side.

He said, "I would be delighted if you came to live with us, and I would be pleased if you wanted that too. But it's your mother I am most concerned about."

He didn't sound like himself. Or not like the Daddy-O I had stayed with at half-term. He didn't even look like him. He was wearing a tweed jacket and cord trousers, the sort of everyday clothes ordinary fathers wear to pick up their kids from school, and his hair wasn't sprayed, and his bald patch was showing.

It was the first time I had been on my own with him. Was that why he was different?

He turned down off the road, into the car park of a country pub, and stopped the car with a jerk. He said, "And Lisa has got to the point in her life when a woman longs for a daughter."

He had said "*a* daughter." Not "*her* daughter."

I could hardly speak. My tongue felt enormous and dry. I croaked, "I'd rather be an orphan."

He nodded. "I hear you, duckie." He leaned across me to open the passenger door and said, "Now I want you to listen to *me*."

We sat in a dark dining room overlooking a field and a river. I wasn't hungry, nor did Daddy-O seem to be, but we both ate a bit, for politeness. I had a Coke and he had half a bottle of wine.

He talked and I listened as he had told me to.

He said perhaps they should never have left me with my grandmother in the first place, but Lisa had had to choose between being an actress and being a mother. Lots of women had jobs and babies, but being in the theater was a special case because you worked in the evenings. That was all right when the child was a baby, because you could take care of it in the daytime, but once it went to school you could never be there to help it with homework or read it bedtime stories.

I wondered why he called the baby "it" instead of "he" or "she." Or "you," because it was me he was talking about. But I thought I had better not interrupt. I took little forkfuls of pink and watery salmon that tasted of nothing at all and washed them down with Coke.

He started on my mother next. She had been sad to leave me and became even sadder as I got older. They had been traveling so much with their company they couldn't see me as often as they would have liked. But she had known I was happy and safe, and that my grandmother loved me.

"That mattered to Lisa," Daddy-O said, suddenly looking stern—almost fierce. "It wasn't only you that she cared about. She cared about her own mother, too. Lisa worried that if we took you away your grandmother would be lonely. She wasn't thinking of herself."

I didn't actually see my mother in the role of suffering martyr. I said, "Gran would be lonely if I went away now. So what's different?"

I *hated* calling her Gran. It didn't suit her. But "my

grandmother" was too fancy to use to my father, and "the Pag" was too personal.

Daddy-O looked at his wineglass. He said, "Your grandmother is an old woman. Too old, your mother thinks, to take care of you properly. You'll say you can take care of yourself, I expect, and I won't quarrel with that, you seem a competent person to me. But think of your gran for a change. If you can."

I stared at him. He took a long swig of his wine and refilled his glass. He still didn't look at me.

He said, "Your gran's worked hard all her life. She deserves a bit of a rest at the end of it. Lisa thinks she does, anyway. Perhaps you ought to ponder on that, young lady, instead of thinking about yourself all the time."

I picked up the bottle of mayonnaise that was supposed to add some sort of flavor to the dead fish in front of me and shook it steadily until it spilled over the plate and dribbled off the edge of the table onto my lap. I jumped up and said, "Oh, what a mess, I'd better go to the ladies' and clean myself up."

And ran, before Daddy-O could say anything. I would have liked to lock myself into a cubicle to cry, but I was afraid he'd come after me. The ladies' was a long, thin room at the back of the building with a sash window that looked out on a cinder path and a wall. The sill was low, the sash went up easily, and I closed it quickly and quietly

168

behind me. I reckoned I had a good ten minutes' start.

The path came out on the far side of the car park. Opposite, there was a gate into a plowed field shielded from the road by a good thick high hedge.

The gate squeaked as I opened it, but once in the shelter of the hedge I was safe for the moment. I ran doubled up, my shoes squelching in the heavy mud, not stopping until I had reached the top of the field and wriggled through another hedge, into a ditch, and out to a narrow lane with grass growing in a line up the middle.

It wasn't much of a road for cars. Perhaps it was only a farm track. But I couldn't risk it, so I went down into the next ditch, among a tangle of stinging nettles, and up through the next hedge into a scraggy piece of land that was part wood, part dump: dead tires and old mattresses abandoned among a few miserable trees and thorny bushes. There was a main road just beyond; I could hear the steady swish of the traffic.

I tried to think what Daddy-O would do, but I didn't know him well enough even to make a guess. I couldn't stay here, in this dreary place. It was freezing, and I had no coat. No money, either, I suddenly realized. My purse was in my school bag, hanging on my hook in the cloakroom.

I trudged uphill through the scrubland, toward the sound of the road. It was a motorway, steep sides freshly planted with little trees and no cover at all. But I was in luck, all the same. A little way along, on my side of the motorway, there was a service station and a fast-food café.

My shoes were heavy with mud. I scraped away as much as I could with handfuls of grass and plodded toward the Happy Eater, keeping below the ridge and out of sight of the road until I was at the back of the service buildings.

There was no one about. It was cold, getting dark, and beginning to rain. There were a few cars in the parking area and in the service station, but no sign of Daddy-O. There would be a telephone inside the café. All I had to do was ring the operator and make a reverse charge call. And pray that the Pag was at home.

Daddy-O had said, "Think of her for a change." He thought I was selfish, expecting the poor old Pag to look after me.

I wanted to cry again. Then I thought, *How thrilled she would be if I called her* poor *and* old, and started to laugh instead as I ran down the bank to the telephone.

Chapter Fifteen

I DIDN'T TELL THE PAG that Daddy-O thought she was too old to look after me. She might have said she agreed with him.

But I told her Daddy-O said I was selfish, only thinking of myself all the time. I couldn't have told her this to her face, I would have been too ashamed. I waited until I was sitting behind her on the bike and shouting into the wind. I felt her back stiffen and I knew she was angry.

She had been angry when she picked me up, swooping into the service station on the bike and looking like Batman with her black leather jacket ballooning behind her and huge goggles to protect her eyes from the wind.

She was angry with my father. She was angry with my

mother. She was even angry with Mrs. Morgan and Mr. Baldry for not standing guard at the school gates to keep kidnappers at bay.

She knew that Daddy-O had whisked me away even before I had telephoned her. Rosie had told Mrs. Morgan and Mrs. Morgan had told Mr. Baldry and Mr. Baldry had rung her at once, and very indignantly. Nobody, not even a parent, was allowed to remove a child from his school during school hours without his permission! He had half a mind to telephone the police!

The Pag said, "I managed to stop that. Though I think your headmaster would have liked to see your father arrested and thrown into prison."

She said, "I do see what you mean about Mr. Baldry. Man's a fool. Gobble gobble like an outraged turkey cock."

She said, "On the other hand, I must admit I wouldn't have minded seeing your father marched off in handcuffs myself!"

She was still angry when we got home. She told me to go upstairs and have a bath. She said, "I'm going into the study to telephone your parents. You are not to listen."

I dawdled on the stairs long enough to hear her talking, though not what she said. Her voice was cold, like wind blowing off ice. It was the same voice that had spoken to Willy Snotnose that afternoon on the station footbridge and scared him half to death. It scared me now. I ran upstairs, humming loudly, and ran a hot, steamy bath.

I had supper in my dressing gown. We had baby lamb chops and spinach. I told her about the disgusting salmon. She said, "Farmed. Never tastes the same. I understand you tried to improve the flavor with mayonnaise."

I said, "I'm surprised you gave him a chance to speak! Let alone enough time to tell tales!"

"I told you not to listen."

"Don't I always do what you tell me? I couldn't help hearing you *speaking*, starting to speak, anyway, but then I hummed so I couldn't hear any *words*."

She said, "Your mother didn't know what he was going to do. I think he meant well."

"You don't sound as if you believe that."

She laughed. Then she looked at me and sighed. She said, "At least he left it to me to tell you. Something in his favor."

"Tell me what?"

She sighed again. She picked up a chop and sucked the last of the meat off the bone. She looked at me. She said, "We have to be at the Family Division of the High Court tomorrow, at ten in the morning."

It was a big, gray building not far from the river. The Pag wanted to walk along the Embankment to "get some fresh air" but I managed to persuade her that breathing in smelly exhaust fumes was not exactly healthy. Besides, it was starting to rain.

"You don't want to catch your death," I said. "Or get all bedraggled so you look like a damp old *crow!*"

I knew this was mean as soon as I'd said it. She was wearing one of her long, traily skirts, but she had pinned the Brooch on her new black jacket and she had put her hair up. I said, "I don't want you to catch cold."

"I never catch colds," was all the Pag said. But she squeezed my hand to show she was not offended.

This time, Mr. Twinkle was there before us, waiting in a cold, square entrance hall. There were security men checking handbags and briefcases but they only glanced at us and nodded us through.

"Dr. Lubonirska," Mr. Twinkle said. He gave a little jump and clicked his heels together, bobbing his head, first at the Pag, then at me. "Miss Catriona Brooke. Ready for the fray? Our judge is in room two hundred and four."

He put his hand under the Pag's elbow and led her out of the entrance hall at a fast trot, and I followed behind them.

A long thin corridor, gray walls, gray carpets, closed doors. Up a flight of stairs and along another corridor that was exactly like the one on the floor below. Each room had a number and the name of a judge, and opposite each door was a padded gray bench.

This corridor was crowded. Most of the people who

were sitting on the benches looked as if they had been there for a long time. Some of them were asleep or just staring into space. Other people stood in small groups, muttering to one another or glancing around them with narrowed and careful expressions as if they were looking for someone they didn't much want to see.

The Pag and I sat on the edge of a bench. Mr. Twinkle said, "A lot of hanging about, I'm afraid. No refreshments, no diversion beyond the human spectacle. Dull for you, Miss Brooke—a chat with the court welfare officer, otherwise a waiting game."

"Don't I see the judge *this* time?"

"I did tell you," the Pag said. "He might ask to see you. But most likely not."

"I was just hoping," I said.

"Television has a lot to answer for," Mr. Twinkle said.

"It's nothing to do with television. It just seems a bit silly, that's all." I gave Mr. Twinkle a chilly look and put on my most sarcastic voice. "It's all supposed to be about me, isn't it? I've got to sit here while you all go and talk to the judge about me and decide about the rest of my life. *My* life, not anyone else's."

"Yes," the Pag said. "That's how it is. You have to trust us."

She glanced past me, along the corridor, and I saw her face twitch. I looked where she looked and saw my mother and father.

All at once I felt dreadful. So sick and shaky and faint I thought I was going to die. I *wished* I could die. Fall down lifeless on the floor and be no more trouble to anyone.

I closed my eyes and pressed myself close to the Pag. I wished I could make myself small enough to creep under her armpit and hide.

The Pag didn't put her arm round me. She just touched my knee, a quick pat, and then took her hand away.

Daddy-O said, "Hello, kiddo," in a friendly voice. I had to look at him then, and he winked at me.

My mother was talking to a woman in a black suit and white blouse. Or she was pretending to be talking. She walked past us without looking at the Pag, or at me. Daddy-O winked again and said, "See you later," speaking softly as if he didn't want my mother to hear him, and then hurried on.

I felt dizzy again. Mr. Twinkle's voice seemed to come from a long way away. "Dr. Lubonirska, I think . . ."

The Pag's bony hand was gripping my arm. She said, "I think we'll have some of that fresh air you were so keen on avoiding."

We stood outside in the drizzling rain. The Pag was grumbling under her breath the way she did sometimes when she was thinking. I said, "I feel silly," and she shook her head as if she were trying to wake herself up.

She said, "You're doing all right."

And put her arm round me at last, and held me until I felt better.

The welfare officer was a jolly lady with a furry face and a loud laugh. We sat in a cold room full of old leather chairs and cardboard boxes tied up with string.

"Papers," she said, guessing what I was thinking. "Papers, papers, papers. No one knows what to do with them. No one wants them but they can't be thrown away either. Now you tell me about yourself, Catriona."

She was easy to talk to. She had a daughter my age and a son a bit older, the same age as Tom. I told her about Rosie and Tom and a bit about school, and the dogs and the cats, and our house in Greece.

She said, "You've lived with your granny for a long time, haven't you?"

"Since I was a baby. Most of my life."

I thought, *She must know this.* She had already talked to the Pag. But she seemed to be waiting.

I said, "I don't want to leave her. Not ever."

She nodded. She said, "How do you feel about going to stay with your mother and father? Just for a visit?"

My mouth was dry. I thought I had to be careful. I said, "I don't mind. I don't mind staying there. I don't mind doing all the *housework*, as long as I can go home at

the end of it." I swallowed but it didn't make any difference, my mouth was still croaky with dryness. I remembered what my very first teacher had said to me, years ago.
I said, "My grandmother is my real family."

They all went into the judge's room, the Pag, Mr.
Twinkle, my mother and Daddy-O and the woman in the
black suit who was their lawyer, and the furry-faced welfare officer.

I sat on the padded bench and waited.

And waited.

I didn't feel sick anymore. I didn't feel anything. I
watched what Mr. Twinkle called "the human spectacle,"
all the other people who were waiting for something—for
one of the judges behind those closed doors to decide
what was going to happen to them.

I tried not to wonder what was going to happen to me.

All the people who were waiting so patiently sat on the
benches, or leaned against the walls, or wandered slowly
along the long, gray corridor, talking to one another in
whispers. No one laughed or cried. They all looked tired
and gray, like the walls, like the carpets.

The only people who seemed to know what they were
there for and what they were doing were the lawyers and
judges: men and women in dark suits and white shirts, hurrying up and down between the waiting people without

seeming to see them, in and out of the rooms, black shoes squeaking, eyelids closing like shutters if anyone made an attempt to stop them or moved to stand in their way.

I thought it was like being on a long, slow train, with no one knowing where it was going or how long it would take. I wished I had brought a book. Or my Game Boy. Even my math homework would have been better than nothing.

The door of the judge's room opened. The first person who came out was my mother. She came toward me, smiling, and when I saw the smile, I thought my heart would stop.

They were going to make me go home with her. The judge had said. "She's your daughter, you can do what you like with her."

I could see the Pag over her shoulder. She was wearing the grim face she puts on when she has to sit in the hall at school functions and is unable to smoke.

My mother said, "It's all settled, my dearest. You are going to have to be a good girl and stay and look after Granny. Daddy-O thinks it would be too *dreadfully* unkind to her to take you away when she's looked after you for so long. But you can come and stay with Daddy-O and me just whenever you want. So don't be *too* sad, my darling."

She put a finger under my chin and lifted it. "Smile for me, precious," she said. "A nice, brave smile for your Mumsie."

I looked at the Pag, but she had raised her eyes to the ceiling. I looked at Daddy-O, and he winked at me.

I smiled for my Mumsie.

And that is almost the end of my story. I stayed with Lisa and Daddy-O for a week in the Easter holidays and had quite a nice time. I went for the summer half-term and took Rosie with me, and while I was away the Pag had Willy to tea and took him for a zoom on the bike. I wasn't altogether pleased about this, but I kept quiet about it.

The Pag and I went to Greece in the summer. We took the bike by motor-rail to cut down the journey because the Pag said she was getting too creaky to drive the whole way. I was pleased about that. Not about the Pag feeling creaky, of course, but because I liked going to sleep with the train rocking under me and waking up in the morning to see the Alps riding past.

It is always hot in Greece in the summer but it was hotter than usual; long, lazy days with the islands offshore looking like sleeping shadows on the flat sea, and the water like glass.

We swam and swam. It was too hot to walk in the mountains.

I wanted to swim to the nearest island.

To begin with, the Pag said, "Wait until you are used to the sea."

Then she said, "Wait until we have bought water shoes in case there are rocks or sea urchins. We'll have to stop and rest on the island, we can't swim there and back in one go."

And she said, "Not today, Cat. Not on top of that huge lunch."

I was used to the sea. We bought plastic water shoes in the village. And one day we didn't have lunch.

It was a beautiful swim. There were no sea urchins lurking round the shore of the island, only small, darting, silver fish in the shallows and little black holes in the sand made by clams breathing under the surface. I tried to dig a few clams for our supper, jabbing my fingers into the breathing holes, but they were always too quick for me, and after a while I lost interest and joined the Pag, who had stretched out on a flat rock in the shade.

She had gone to sleep, and I went to sleep, too. When we woke the wind had come up, only enough to wrinkle the water a little, but there was a fat black cloud resting on top of the mountain, and the wind was behind it.

We stretched and yawned and went into the sea. It was lovely and silky, and the sun danced in bright, jagged points on the ruffly waves. We had the bay to ourselves, no boats on the sea, no one in sight on the land.

It was a long way to the beach, and halfway there I was bored. "Let's play monsters," I called out to the Pag, who was swimming behind me. This was a childish game we had often played when I was much younger: the Pag pretending to be a shark or a whale, chasing me through the water and growling. (I knew sharks and whales didn't growl, even when I was little, but growling made it more scary.)

The Pag shook her head without speaking. Her gray hair was streaming around her like seaweed. I thought her face looked paler than usual, but the sun drains out color sometimes so I couldn't be sure. She smiled and waved at me, meaning *Pay no attention*. And turned on her back.

I swam to her. Her legs were kicking quite strongly but her arms were trailing in the water. She was puffing a bit.

She said, "I'm fine. Go on in. I'll come slowly."

I could see she would fuss if I didn't do what she told me. And fussing would tire her.

I swam ahead. Not too far, and looking back every two or three seconds. I could hear her grunting each time she kicked, as if kicking was becoming a terrible effort.

It was still quite a way to the shore.

I turned to watch her, treading water.

The water was rougher now, bumping my chin and splashing into my mouth. And the black cloud was spreading over the sky. As I watched, it touched the edge of the sun, turning it watery.

She began to thrash about with her arms. She seemed to be choking. I shouted, "Hold on, Pag, I'm coming."

I tried to get hold of her. She pushed me away. She gasped painfully, "No, no, silly girl, no."

I said, "Then we'll both drown, you silly old woman."

All the same, I wasn't sure I could save her. Although she was thin, she was taller than me, and much heavier. I had practiced for my Lifesaving Badge on a girl who was lighter and smaller—and in a calm swimming pool.

I could see she was frightened, and that frightened me. But she managed to keep still, no struggling, no fighting, and I pushed her and pulled her, trying this way and that way, keeping her head out of the sea, sometimes on my chest as I swam on my back, sometimes on my shoulder as I swam sidestroke, one arm wrapped around her, thinking about nothing except *getting there*, to the white beach that was gray now under the dark sky. And still so far away.

She started to cough. The choke turned into a strange, whooping laugh. I thought she was panicking, pushing my hands away, sinking down in the water, then I realized she was standing. She was so much taller, she had touched bottom long before me.

We staggered to the beach, supporting each other. The sea hissed on the white stones and we fell into the surf. I crawled the last few yards to the land and turned back to help her.

She was under the water, face downward, not moving. I grabbed her under her armpits and tugged until I thought my lungs would burst and my arms tear from their sockets.

The sea frilled and ebbed round her legs, but her body was safe on the stones of the beach. She was lying on her front. I turned her head sideways. Her eyes were closed.

I said, *"Pag!"*

She didn't move. Her lips were the color of stone. I knelt beside her. I said, "Don't die, please don't die, not now, not this year, anyway, not till I'm older, please, oh, please. . . ."

I knew I ought to do something to make her breathe. Instead, I started to cry. There was salt sea in my mouth, in my nose, in my tears.

She coughed. Sea dribbled out of her mouth. She got on her hands and knees and coughed and coughed and coughed. She looked at me through her long, gray fringe of hair and tried to smile with her gray lips.

Her breath came in little, hoarse flutters. "If I'm to hang around till you're grown"—cough, puff, and sob—"I'll have to stop smoking."

And she did.